'Now, listen up, Stacy,' Amanda said. 'You're going to be eleven in a week or so. It's about time you started taking an interest in how you look.'

'I like the way I look,' I said.

'But we could make you look so much better,' Amanda said.

'We?' I said. 'Who's *we*? You don't really think I'd let Cheryl and Rachel and Natalie give me a makeover? I'd wind up looking like something from a Halloween party.'

Amanda caught hold of my hand and towed me across the floor.

'Come *on*, Stacy,' she said. 'An hour with Madame Amanda and you won't recognize yourself.'

'That's what I'm afraid of,' I said as Amanda yanked me along the hall.

Amanda opened her bedroom door and marched me in ahead of her.

The three Bimbos looked at me.

'Girls,' Amanda said, 'we've got some work to do!'

Little Sister books published by Red Fox

LITTLE SISTER

The New Stacy

Allan Frewin Jones

**Series created by
Ben M. Baglio**

RED FOX

A Red Fox Book

Published by Random House Children's Books
20 Vauxhall Bridge Road, London SW1V 2SA

A division of Random House UK Ltd
London Melbourne Sydney Auckland
Johannesburg and agencies throughout the world

1 3 5 7 9 10 8 6 4 2

First published in Great Britain by Red Fox 1996

Set in 12/14 Plantin by Intype London Ltd

Printed and bound in Great Britain by
Cox & Wyman Ltd, Reading, Berkshire

Papers used by Random House UK Ltd are natural, recyclable
products made from wood grown in sustainable forests. The
manufacturing processes conform to the environmental regulations
of the country of origin.

RANDOM HOUSE UK Limited Reg No. 954009

ISBN 0 09 966651 0

Chapter One

'Stacy! Will you get off that phone! I have to make a really important call!'

My thirteen-year-old sister Amanda was standing in the middle of the hall in her robe with her fists on her hips and her wet hair in a plastic bag.

Question: Why is my sister Amanda wearing a plastic bag on her head?

Answer: Because she's trying to keep all the *air* in her head from escaping.

Actually, she was in the middle of tinting her hair with some dye stuff called 'Golden Sunshine'. Her hair is already blonde – but Amanda had decided that it wasn't blonde *enough*. It needed to be just a little *blonder*.

My sister is like that. Amanda's big ambitions in life are to have blonder and curlier hair, bluer and brighter eyes, a whiter and wider smile and boobs that will actually fill the new bra she bought the other week.

But Amanda isn't the only one in our house with ambitions.

Allen Family Ambitions

Mom: To publish a book of poetry. (Mom's real job is proofreading book manuscripts, but she makes a little money from writing greeting-card rhymes.)

Dad: To find a job that means he doesn't have to travel all the way to Chicago almost every weekday.

Baby Sam: to take two steps without falling over.

My cat Benjamin: to catch one of those sparrows that he spends half his life chasing around up on the roof.

And me? Well, right then my ambition was to finish talking to my best friend, Cindy Spiegel, without Amanda standing over me glaring and dripping on me and telling me to get off the phone.

Cindy and her whole family had just moved to California. My family and I live in Four Corners, Indiana. California is hundreds and hundreds of miles away, which is why calls to my far-away best friend are kind of important to me. And that was why I was getting cheesed off with Amanda.

'Quit bothering me,' I said. 'Dad said I could call Cindy.'

'Is Amanda being a pain?' Cindy asked from the other end of the phone.

'She sure is!' I said, giving Amanda a mega-glare.

'I sure am *what*?' Amanda demanded. 'What's she saying about me?'

'Just a moment, Cindy,' I said. I put my hand over the mouthpiece. 'I only get to talk to Cindy once a week,' I said to Amanda. 'So I'd be really grateful if you could get lost!'

'But I need to talk to Cheryl,' Amanda whined. 'I can't find the instructions from the pack of hair-dye. I need to know how long I have to stay like this.' She waved her hand at the plastic bag covering her hair.

'Cindy might know,' I said. I took my hand away from the mouthpiece. 'Cindy? Have you ever used "Golden Sunshine" hair-dye?'

'Nope,' Cindy said. 'Why?'

'Uh-huh?' I said, pretending Cindy was telling me things. 'I see. Yup. Yeah, I've got it.'

'Stacy,' Cindy said, 'didn't you hear me? I said I've never used it.'

'Sure I did,' I said. 'Yeah, I'll tell her.' I looked up at Amanda. 'For a start,' I told her, 'Cindy says you're not wearing the plastic bag right. It should cover your whole head and it

7

should be tied around your neck with a rubber band.'

Amanda stared at me. 'Is she some kind of nut?' she asked. 'I wouldn't be able to *breathe*!'

I grinned at her. 'No pain, no gain, Amanda.'

'Wait a minute!' Amanda howled. 'How does *she* know how I'm wearing the bag?' It had taken a few seconds, but Amanda had figured out that I was making fun of her. 'You creep!'

She grabbed at me and we wrestled for the phone.

'Amanda!' I shrieked. 'Your *hair*!'

She was on top of me on the stairs, pinning me down.

'What?' she panted.

'It's turned green!' I yelled, staring at it.

'Oh, right,' Amanda said. 'I really believe you, Stacy.'

'Amanda,' I said, 'trust me on this. If you never trust me ever again, trust me *this* time. Your hair has turned *green*!'

It hadn't really, but I must have put on a really convincing act. Amanda let out a panicky wail and flew up the stairs to the bathroom.

'Stacy?' Cindy was calling. 'Hello? What's going on?'

'I was just getting rid of a pest,' I told her.

There was an angry bellow from the bathroom.

'I think the pest is about to come back,' I said to Cindy. 'I'd better get out of here. Call me next Sunday, OK?'

'I sure will,' Cindy said. 'Same time?'

'Yup. Same time, same channel,' I said. Amanda came bursting out of the bathroom. 'Ohmygosh!' I said. 'I gotta go, Cindy. Bye.'

I put the phone down and ran for the front door as Amanda came charging down the stairs to get me.

I was lucky that the door was open, or she'd have caught me in the hall and torn me to tiny little pieces. Dad was working on the car in the driveway.

'Hi, Dad,' I said as I zipped past him. 'Bye, Dad.' He lifted his head from under the raised hood.

I glanced over my shoulder as I hit the side-walk. Amanda was only a couple of yards behind me. The belt of her robe was coming loose as she ran.

I turned on my heel and waved my arms at her.

'Amanda!' I yelled. 'You don't have any underwear on!'

Amanda took a look down at her half-open robe.

'Eeek!' She wrapped the robe tight around herself and vanished back into the house like a rocket.

The last thing I heard was: 'I'll get you for this, Stacy. Just you wait!'

I walked back up our driveway.

Dad shook his head.

'What was all that about?' he asked.

'I was trying to talk to Cindy and Amanda was being a pain,' I told him.

Mom was out with Sam, visiting Grandma and Grandpa Whittle.

I peered around the semi-open front door. Amanda was sitting on the stairs, talking on the phone.

'OK,' she was saying. (She was obviously talking to Cheryl.) 'So I keep this stuff on for thirty minutes and then rinse my hair thoroughly and that's *it*, yeah?'

I ran for the stairs and managed to zip up past Amanda without her catching hold of me.

I headed for my room. Benjamin was asleep in Donovan's lap. Benjamin is a pedigree cat – a Russian Blue with green eyes and sleek grey fur. Donovan is a huge blue and white stuffed rabbit that my Aunt Susie left here for us to look after. Donovan isn't a pedigree rabbit *at all*; he's a big, ugly, dumb-looking *mess*! But Benjamin seems to be really comfortable in his lap.

I sat at my desk and read through the letter I had just received from Cindy. There were some pictures of her new house in San Diego. And pictures of a long yellow beach and palm trees and big white houses. Cindy said it was only a two-minute walk from her new house to the beach.

An Interesting Fact

From the centre of the town where I live, at a walking speed of four miles an hour (which is pretty fast), it would take me two weeks, two days and sixteen hours to get to the same beach! And it takes Cindy *two minutes*. I ask you – is that *fair*?

(PS *Statistics worked out by my friend Pippa Kane, who knows stuff like that.*)

I sighed as I spread the pictures out on my desk. One of them was of Cindy kneeling on her bed in her new bedroom. All her things were around her. On the wall behind her was the cat calendar that I had bought her last Christmas.

I was missing Cindy an awful lot! You don't realize how much you need your best friend until she isn't there any more. Letters and calls and pictures are OK, but they don't make up for the fact that I can't see Cindy whenever I want to.

Pippa Kane and Fern Kipsak are really special friends of mine, too, and we do a lot of stuff together, but Cindy was my all-time best friend. And now she's in California and I'm stuck in Four Corners feeling totally fed up!

I went downstairs. I could hear water running in the bathroom. Amanda was rinsing out her *even-blonder* hair.

It would be funny if it really did turn green!

I wondered if James would like her if she had green hair. James is Amanda's boyfriend. He's really nice: I don't know *what* he sees in a total airhead like Amanda.

Mom had been doing some major sorting out in the living-room cabinet. There was a box of stuff to be thrown out and a second box of things that she was going to put down in the basement.

On top of the second box was an old picture album. I really like looking at old pictures. I tucked the album under my arm and headed back up to my room.

I sat on the bed with the album in my lap. I opened the album and saw a picture of

Amanda and me walking down the gangplank of a ship. It was called the *Calypso*. A whole load of memories came flooding back as I sat looking at that picture.

It had been taken on vacation in the Florida Keys, three years ago. Amanda was ten and I was seven. (Nowadays Amanda is thirteen and *I'm* ten – although my eleventh birthday was coming up real soon.)

I turned the page. In the next picture Amanda and I were standing on the dock together. Amanda had one arm around my shoulders and we were both smiling and waving into the camera.

For the *millionth* time I wondered why Amanda had wavy blonde hair, blue eyes and a big perfect smile, while I had boring brown hair, a face full of freckles and the kind of smile that meant I needed a brace on my teeth.

I was just about to turn the next page when Benjamin jumped up on to the bed and sat right down in the middle of the album.

'*Mroop*,' he said. Which means, 'Hello. I've just woken up. Pet me *now*!'

I slid the album from under Benjamin and petted him while I looked at some more vacation pictures from three years ago.

'It's kind of strange,' I said to Benjamin. 'Amanda and I used to do things together all the time back then. We used to share a room – you won't remember that, Benjamin, you weren't around then – and we used to play games together and talk a whole lot. Sometimes Mom would have to come in three or four times to tell us to quiet down and go to sleep.'

I frowned down at the old pictures of Amanda and me having fun together. What had happened? How come we weren't like that any more?

'Maybe it's because Amanda is too busy pretending to be all grown-up these days,' I said to Benjamin. 'It sure isn't *my* fault.'

Benjamin just looked at me.

'Amanda is a pest,' I said to him. I looked at the pictures again and sighed. I was wondering what would happen if I put a little more effort into being friendly with her. Would she start being friendly back?

'You know what, Benjamin,' I said. 'I'm going to make a real effort to be nice to Amanda from now on. And then maybe we can get back to being really good friends like we used to be. What do you say?'

'*Bruurp*,' Benjamin said, which I think meant, '*Good idea.*'

My bedroom door burst open and a sopping wet sponge came flying across the room.

Benjamin was under the bed in a split second as the sponge splatted against my T-shirt and covered me with soapy water.

'That's for being a stupid nerdy little creep and telling me my hair had turned green!' Amanda yelled as she ducked out and slammed the door again.

'*Gruuurgh!*' I spluttered through a mouthful of soap as I clawed foam out of my eyes.

It looked like my decision to be nice to Amanda was going to be a whole lot harder to stick to than I'd thought! Just then the only thought in my head was *revenge*!

Chapter Two

Amanda barricaded herself in her room after throwing the soapy sponge at me.

But I could wait. I hadn't lived with Amanda for ten years without learning to be patient. She'd have to come out of that room sometime, and when she did I would be waiting with that sponge. I loaded it with more water from the bathroom. It meant I was getting even wetter, but the moment Amanda's head appeared, that sponge was going to land: *splatoozie*! right in her mouth.

I got bored with the whole thing after about ten minutes.

'I have better things to do than sit out here!' I yelled through the door. 'I don't care if you *never* come out! In fact, I'd prefer it!'

I left the sponge on the floor. Amanda had taken it out of the bathroom, so *she* could put it back!

I went back to my room but I didn't feel like looking at the old pictures again, so I put the album back in the box and spent some time outside watching Dad while he worked on the car.

Mom and baby Sam arrived home about an hour later. Mom had stopped off to buy a big carton of ice-cream.

Dad called Amanda down and we all sat out front eating the ice-cream. I stuck my tongue out at Amanda when Mom and Dad weren't looking and she stuck her tongue out at me, but apart from that we mostly ignored each other.

Mom and Dad complimented Amanda on her new hair colour. (If you ask me, it looked exactly the same!)

I sat Sam on my lap and helped him get most of the ice-cream in his mouth rather than over his face and down his clothes.

(It's a strange thing about helping Sam with his food. You might *think* most of it ends up in his mouth, but you keep discovering chunks and splats of food all over yourself for hours afterwards.)

A little later Amanda went off to meet James and I took Sam inside to play. Mom came into the living room with her needlepoint. She had only just sat down when the phone rang.

It was for her. I heard her voice sounding more and more annoyed as she spoke and in the end she slammed the phone down and let out an angry yell.

'Mom?' I called. 'Is something wrong?'

'It's Sunday afternoon!' she said. 'I shouldn't have to work on a Sunday afternoon!'

It turned out that the call had been from one of the publishers she works for. (Her job is to make sure book manuscripts have all the right spelling and grammar, and that everything makes sense before they get published.) Anyway, there was some kind of emergency which meant Mom had to get some work done by first thing tomorrow morning.

The reason I'm telling you this is because it helps explain why Mom was in such a bad mood later that day. And her mood didn't get any better when she went upstairs and found a wet sponge on the floor outside Amanda's bedroom door, and a big water stain on the carpet.

'Stacy!'

I jumped up and ran to see what the problem was. Mom had called '*Stacy!*' in a voice that means '*Get up here NOW!*'

'Do you know why this was lying here?' she asked, holding the sponge out.

'Oh! I forgot it!' I said. 'But it wasn't my fault. It was Amanda.'

'Amanda dropped it here?'

'Uh, no . . .'

'Then who did? The *cat*?' I knew Mom wouldn't have reacted this badly if she wasn't already in a foul mood; but that didn't help much right then.

'I did,' I admitted.

'Do you have any idea how difficult it is to get a dried-in water stain out of a carpet, Stacy?' Mom said.

'Amanda threw it at me,' I said. 'I didn't start it. Honest, I didn't!'

'Oh, for heaven's sake, Stacy,' Mom snapped. 'I wish you'd grow up! Sometimes you sound like a six-year-old!'

That really hurt! I ran to my room and threw myself on my bed.

A little while later Mom came in to say sorry and to give me a whole heap of cuddles. Then I said I was sorry about the sponge. And then Mom said it wasn't a big deal and she shouldn't have blown her top at *me* just because the idiots she was working for right then were giving her a hard time.

And I said, do I really behave like a six-year-old sometimes? And Mom said, no, I was just angry.

'You behave like a very smart ten-year-old,' Mom said, giving me another cuddle.

'But I'm going to be eleven next week,' I said. 'I don't want to behave like a smart ten-year-old when I'm eleven. And it's only a week away.' I looked at her. 'I'm going to make a real effort to act like a smart eleven-year-old from now on.'

'Don't try to be *too* grown-up too quickly,' Mom said. 'People who try to *act* grown-up are usually the most childish.'

(Yeah, I thought, take a look at Amanda. She desperately wants to be eighteen, and half the time she behaves like she's around Sam's age!)

That night in bed I made a solemn resolution.

Stacy's Solemn Resolution

I resolve that from now on I am going to be the NEW IMPROVED STACY. If things go wrong, I will not blame other people – not even if it IS Amanda's fault. I will behave at all times in a sensible and thoughtful way. I will do my best to behave towards Amanda like an adult, even though she can be totally infuriating and has the brains of a balloon!

Signed by Stacy Allen.

Witnessed by Benjamin.

PS May my teeth stay permanently crooked

*and may I never eat chocolate chip ice-cream
again if I do not keep to this Solemn Resolution!*

Chapter Three

We were sitting in class on Monday morning.
As usual, Fern and Pippa were sitting behind
me.

Fern was whispering something to Pippa. I
couldn't quite hear what she was saying. It
sounded like she was talking about something
called a *rice gun*.

'What's a rice gun?' I hissed.

'*Price* gun,' Fern whispered, 'not *rice* gun.
It's the thing we use in the store to put price
tags on everything.' (Fern's mom and dad run
a general store.) 'I'm helping out now and
then in the store, stacking shelves and pricing
stuff up,' Fern said. 'Mom and Dad are putting my wages away for me so I'll have a whole
heap of vacation money saved.'

'Fern!' Ms Fenwick said sharply. 'Settle
down and keep quiet. And Stacy – keep your
eyes to the front, please.'

I turned to face front. I like Ms Fenwick
although she's pretty strict with us. She's got

eagle eyes that can see *everything*, and special *teacher* ears that can hear even the quietest whisper.

'Now, then,' Ms Fenwick said, 'we're going to be starting an exciting new project today.' She turned and wrote on the board. It was a name. Charles Darwin.

'Does anyone know who Charles Darwin was?' Ms Fenwick asked.

'Doesn't he play the part of the grandfather in *Spindrift*?' Fern called out. (*Spindrift* is our favourite TV soap opera.)

'If you can't be sensible, Fern, be quiet!' Ms Fenwick said. 'Anyone else?'

'I thought I *was* being sensible,' Fern mumbled under her breath.

'The guy you're thinking of is Charles Dawson,' I hissed.

Meanwhile, Pippa and Betsy-Jane Garside had both put their hands up. Pippa is really brainy, but Betsy-Jane is just a show-off.

'Betsy-Jane?' Ms Fenwick asked.

'He was the man who invented *evolution*,' Betsy Jane said with this sickeningly smug look on her face.

Pippa bounced up and down in her seat. 'Ms Fenwick! Ms Fenwick!'

'Yes, Pippa?'

'Charles Darwin didn't *invent* evolution,'

Pippa said. 'He just figured it out after seeing some strange animals on an island somewhere in the Pacific Ocean.' Pippa shot Betsy-Jane a triumphant look.

'That's an excellent answer, Pippa,' Ms Fenwick said. Betsy-Jane looked like she was sucking on a lemon.

'How do you *know* these things?' Fern hissed at Pippa.

'I guess my mom must have told me,' Pippa said. Pippa's mom is a college professor.

Ms Fenwick wrote *Evolution* on the board. 'After visiting the Galapagos Islands, Charles Darwin put together his theory of evolution.'

It's not every day that we get to hear in class about stuff that interests me, but I like anything to do with nature studies and animals. As Ms Fenwick explained about Charles Darwin's theories I sat there listening to every word she said.

Basically, this *evolution* stuff was all about how animals changed to fit in with their changing surroundings. These changes, Ms Fenwick told us, took hundreds of thousands of years.

'And some species of animals didn't manage to change,' Ms Fenwick said. 'And they died out altogether. Does anyone know what a mammoth was?'

I put my hand up. There had been an article in my wildlife magazine only last month all about extinct animals – including mammoths.

'They were like big hairy elephants,' I said. 'They lived during the Ice Age. They're all dead now.'

'Very good, Stacy.' Ms Fenwick wrote *Animals Adapt to Survive* on the board.

'Now, then,' she said, 'we're going to do some more work on this in class, but what I want you to do is to pair off for homework projects on the subject of how animals change to survive in a changing world.'

Brilliant! A project about animals. Like always, I'd pair up with Cindy, and the two of us would . . .

HOLD IT! WAIT A MINUTE! STOP THE TRAFFIC!

How could I pair up with Cindy? Cindy was in California.

I looked around the class to try and find someone to team up with. Larry Franco was sitting nearest, but he always turned bright red and hid in a corner if a girl even *spoke* to him.

Then there was Betsy-Jane, but she always paired up with Sophie Carpenter, who is the dumbest girl in our class.

Fern and Pippa had already teamed up. What was I supposed to do? Who was I going to end up with? Not Rosie Pilcher, please! She was a walking disaster area. A person could get themselves *killed* just by standing next to her. (Right then, Rosie had her arm in a cast because she'd fallen down after stepping on a banana peel! Honest! I know that *never* happens to normal people, but Rosie just isn't normal.)

I breathed a sigh of relief when I saw Rosie go and sit next to Peter Bolger.

'Ms Fenwick,' I said, 'I don't have anyone to work with.'

'Is there anyone else without a partner?' Ms Fenwick asked. 'Is there anyone to pair up with Stacy?'

There wasn't. When Cindy had been here, there had been an even number of people in our class. Now she was gone, there was an odd number. And the odd one out was *me*!

'You can join us,' Pippa said.

That seemed like a good idea. When Cindy had been here, the four of us had always hung around together, and we'd even done projects together in the past, although when it came to pairs it had always been Cindy and me.

At lunchtime we sat at our usual table in the cafeteria and made plans. For a start, we needed to decide whose house we would work in. Pippa and I lived the furthest apart. Fern lived almost midway between us. So it made sense for us to meet up at Fern's house.

'I'll take the bus home,' I told them, 'pick up the magazine that has all the stuff about extinct animals in it, and ride my bike over.'

'OK,' Pippa said, 'and I'll see if my mom has any books we could use.'

'This is going to be great,' I said. 'A project all about animals! I can't wait to start!'

* * *

When I arrived at Fern's house, Pippa was already there. The two of them were playing with Lucky, our jointly owned puppy. He's only three months old, but he's getting to look like a regular dog and he's always chewing something up.

I walked into Fern's room to find Pippa sitting on the floor playing tug of war with Lucky over a chomped-up old slipper.

'Hi, Stacy,' Pippa said, letting go of her end of the slipper. Lucky went head over heels across the floor and we all laughed at the surprised look on his face.

We played with Lucky for a while; throwing his slipper in the air to make him jump or spinning it across the floor so he'd go running after it. He usually fell over in a tangle of ears and paws and a madly wagging tail.

'I think maybe we'd better take a look at the project,' I said. We'd been playing with Lucky for ages and he didn't show any signs of slowing down.

Pippa pulled a thick book out of her bag.

'This has all the information we'll need,' she said. 'It's got a whole chapter on Darwin.'

Fern was lying on her back, wriggling and squirming and laughing as Lucky licked her face.

'Including evolution and the adapting to survive thing?' Fern asked.

'Yup,' Pippa said. She pulled her notebook out of her bag. She stretched out on the carpet, opened the big book she had brought with her, and started writing in her notebook. Fern was rolling around on the floor with Lucky and he was pretend-growling and worrying at the raggy old slipper.

I stared at Pippa for a few seconds.

'What are you writing?' I asked.

'The title,' Pippa said. She read it out: ' "Charles Darwin's Theories of Evolution and the Survival of the Fittest. By Pippa Kane, Fern Kipsak and Stacy Allen".'

'What's *survival of the fittest* mean?' Fern asked.

'It means all the brainy animals survive, and all the dumb ones get killed off,' Pippa said.

'Something like that, anyway.' Then she read a few lines from the big book, stuck her tongue out of the corner of her mouth and started writing again.

' "Charles Darwin was an English naturalist," ' she said aloud as she wrote. ' "He was born in – " '

'Excuse me!' I said loudly.

Pippa looked up at me. 'Huh?'

'What are you *doing*?' I asked.

'Our *project*,' Pippa said. 'What does it look like I'm doing?'

'But we haven't talked about it at all,' I said. 'And you haven't even *looked* at my magazine.'

Pippa looked puzzled. She sat up. 'OK,' she said. 'Show me your magazine.'

I handed it over to her. There was a whole double-page spread on the Ice Age (which was when mammoths lived). There was even a story about a mammoth that had been frozen in ice for thousands of years.

'Nice pictures,' Pippa said. 'Can we cut them out and use them?'

'No way,' I said. 'I collect these magazines. I don't want big holes cut out of them.'

Pippa shrugged. 'OK,' she said. She handed the magazine back and started writing again.

'Excuse me *again*,' I said. 'What's going on

here? Aren't we supposed to work on this together?'

'It's quicker like this,' Pippa explained. 'I can get the whole thing done in half the time if Fern keeps out of my way.'

Fern grinned as she tossed the slipper for Lucky. 'That's fine with me,' she said.

'What about *me*?' I asked. 'What do I get to do?'

Pippa looked up at me. 'Look,' she said, 'there's only one book, OK? And only one of us needs to write stuff down. Maybe you could – ' she waved her arm vaguely ' – go find some drawing paper and copy that picture of the mammoth. We could use a few pictures.'

'I can't draw,' I reminded her. 'Besides, I want to help decide what we're going to put. I'm not going to just sit here while you copy stuff out of a book!'

'I am not copying,' Pippa sounded really offended. 'I am *paraphrasing*.'

'You know I don't know what that means!' I said, getting annoyed.

'Lighten up,' Fern said. 'Pippa *likes* doing all the work.' She sat up with Lucky rolling around in her lap. 'We've got a really good partnership here.'

'Well, when I teamed up with Cindy, we used to work *together*,' I said.

'Cindy's in San Diego,' Pippa said.

'You don't have to tell *me* that!' I said snappily. 'I really wish she wasn't! At least she wouldn't have taken a ten-second look at my magazine and then totally *ignored* it.'

'All that stuff is in my book,' Pippa said.

'So what am I *doing* here?' I asked. 'I should have just stayed home.'

Pippa sat up again. 'Look, Stacy, who has the neatest handwriting of the three of us?'

'You do, I guess,' I said.

'And who has a mother who is a college professor?' Fern asked.

'What's that got to do with anything?' I asked.

'Pippa is brainier than you,' Fern said. 'Why don't you just let her do it?'

I took a deep breath.

'I think maybe I'll work on this project on my own,' I said. 'You guys just go ahead and do your thing.' I picked up my magazine. 'You obviously don't need *me*.'

'Stacy, don't be so silly,' Pippa said. 'Sit down.'

'Oh, right!' I said. 'My magazine is useless. My writing isn't neat enough for you. My mom isn't a professor, and I don't have a big book with *everything* in the *world* written in it.

31

And now I'm silly, too, huh? Well, *thanks*, Pippa. You're a real friend.'

I stormed out and ran down the stairs. I was really angry but I wasn't going back, even if both of them came running after me and begged!

I grabbed my bike and went down to the sidewalk. I listened for some sound of them following me. I glared up at Fern's window. So! They weren't even going to apologize! *That* was how much my friendship meant to them. They couldn't even be bothered to come down and stop me cycling off!

Talk about unreasonable people! I cycled home.

'Mom?' I called. 'Have there been any calls for me?'

'No, honey,' Mom said. She came out of the kitchen. 'You're back early,' she said. 'Did you get everything done?'

'Not exactly,' I said as I headed up the stairs. 'I've decided I work better on my own.' I looked down at her. 'And if Pippa or Fern call, tell them I'm not home!'

Chapter Four

I sat at my desk and got my notebook out. I wrote: *Charles Darwin's Theories of Evolution and the Survival of the Fittest, by Stacy Allen.* Then I sat for a few minutes, sucking the end of my pen and thinking about the title.

'No way,' I said to myself. 'That was Pippa's title. I'm going to come up with something different.'

I crossed it out and wrote: *The Survival of the Fittest, by Stacy Allen.*

Yeah, that was better.

I kept listening for the phone. I was sure that Pippa or Fern would call me to apologize.

There was a knock on the door and Mom came in with a pile of newly folded clothes.

'Sorry to disturb you while you're working, honey,' Mom said. 'How's it going?'

'Fine,' I said, casually resting my arms right across my notebook so Mom couldn't see that I hadn't written a single thing other than the title.

'So how come you aren't working with Pippa and Fern after all?' Mom asked.

'I think I work better on my own,' I said.

Mom sat on my bed. 'I see,' she said. She gave me one of her *knowing* looks. 'Do you want to tell me what happened?'

'What makes you think anything happened?' I asked.

'Oh, just a little thing like you not wanting to talk to them if they call,' Mom said.

'Pippa thinks she's so smart!' I blurted out. 'And Fern just wants to mess around. They didn't even look at my magazine. Pippa just turned up with some *book* and started writing the project as if I wasn't even there. Cindy never used to do that. We used to work *together.*'

'Come here,' Mom said. I went and sat next to her and she gave me a big hug. 'I know it's hard for you to get used to being without Cindy,' she said. 'But you can't spend the rest of your life moping and being miserable about it.'

'Yes I can,' I mumbled.

'Well, yes, you *can*,' Mom said with a smile. 'But you *mustn't*, Stacy. You can't keep on thinking how things *used* to be. And you really can't blame Pippa and Fern for not being

Cindy. That just isn't fair on them. You've got to accept things the way they are.'

'I guess so,' I said.

'I'm not telling you what to do,' Mom said. 'But if I were you, I'd want to make up with Pippa and Fern.' She stood up. 'At least think about it, huh?'

I nodded.

Maybe Mom was right. To be honest, the more I thought about the argument I'd had with Pippa, the *dumber* I felt. And how long was it since I'd decided to act totally grown-up?

A grown-up Stacy would have talked the problem through with Pippa and Fern. A grown-up Stacy would have come to some *agreement* with them. A grown-up Stacy would be at Fern's house right now, working on that project.

I decided to make peace with them first thing tomorrow.

I felt a whole lot better once I'd sorted all that out in my head.

The all-new, super-grown-up Stacy was going to make sure that everything worked out just fine.

* * *

Things didn't go exactly according to plan the

next morning. I sat next to Fern on the school bus, but she wasn't interested in talking about anything other than the work she was doing in her folks' store. I found out everything a person could *possibly* want to know about how to load and use a pricing gun, but I didn't get a chance to ask her about how the project was going. (When Fern starts talking, it's sometimes kind of hard to get a word in.)

I didn't see Pippa out by the lockers. In fact, Pippa didn't come to homeroom until the very last second. She came in with Andy Melniker.

Andy's OK, but Pippa had never shown any interest in talking to him before, so I was kind of surprised to see them together like that.

I gave Pippa a big smile, but she didn't even seem to see me.

Maybe she was still annoyed from yesterday afternoon. Well, the new-improved Stacy could deal with that.

I turned around in my chair and beamed Pippa another smile.

'How is the project going?' I asked. 'I'm sorry I acted like a little kid about it yesterday.'

'Huh?' Pippa was staring into space like I wasn't even there. 'Oh, right. Forget it.'

I couldn't believe it! I'd apologized. I'd given her a big smile and I'd tried to make up, like any normal grown-up person would, and Pippa was as good as *ignoring* me!

Ms Fenwick called for quiet. Well, as far as talking to Pippa Kane was concerned, Ms Fenwick could have all the quiet from *me* that she wanted. I wasn't going to say another word to her. I'd tried to make up. If she wasn't interested, then that was her problem. I sure wasn't going to lose any sleep over it!

Things didn't improve over lunch. Pippa didn't sit at our usual table. In fact, Pippa didn't even show up in the cafeteria at all. I mean, I've heard of people sulking, but Pippa was making a really big deal out of this.

Fern was sitting at our table, scribbling stuff on some scrap paper when I went over with my tray.

'Hi,' I said, super-cheerfully. I sat down. 'Have you seen Pippa?'

Fern didn't even look up from her scribbling. 'Yeah,' she said.

'So where is she?' I asked.

'Beats me,' Fern said.

'But you said you'd seen her,' I said.

'I have. Plenty of times.' She finally looked up at me. 'But not *recently*. Are you any good at math?'

I looked at the scribbling Fern had been doing. It was a whole bunch of numbers with loads of crossings out and multiplications and divisions.

'A *little*,' I said. 'Why?'

'I'm trying to figure out how much money I'll end up with if I work in the store until summer vacation,' Fern said. She started talking about dollars per hour, and hours per week, and weeks per month and how much she'd lose if she only worked one afternoon a week instead of two.

I felt like saying, *Fern, shut up, this is more boring to listen to that you could possibly imagine.*

But I didn't say that. I just sat there and listened to Fern going on about how much money she was going to make and what she planned on doing with it.

And that was how I spent lunch that day. Being bored to little pieces by Fern.

I spotted Pippa and Andy together again later, but when I went over to give Pippa one last chance to make friends, the two of them walked off together as if they hadn't even seen me. (They must have seen me – I might be small, but I'm not *invisible*!)

Great! I knew when I wasn't wanted. Pippa had a new friend. Well, that was just fine with me. And Fern was so busy with her brilliant new career in her parents' store that I might as well try having a conversation with lemon Jell-O!

I thought about a particular sentence that had stuck in my mind from the article about mammoths: *As the living conditions began to change around them, animals were given a stark choice: adapt or die.*

Well, *my* living conditions were sure changing around me! No kidding they were! Cindy was gone, Fern was totally obsessed with calculating how much vacation money she was going to make, and Pippa was spending all her time with Andy Melniker.

And on top of *that*, I was going to be eleven in one and a half weeks.

If all that didn't count as *changing living conditions*, I'd like to know what did!

The question was: what was I going to do about it?

⋆　⋆　⋆

I thought about it all week. Pippa and Fern hardly spoke to me and I hardly spoke to them, so I had plenty of time to do some hard thinking. And I was still thinking about it by the weekend.

Actually, that Saturday morning wasn't the best time for me to try and do any serious thinking.

Why? Because my sister had invited her three best Bimbo friends over and the four of them were in her room listening to loud music and yelling and screeching with laughter the way the Bimbo Brigade always does when it gets together.

Boom, boom, boom, boom, went the music through my wall.

Screech, cackle, yell, holler, went the Bimbos.

I started writing a letter to Cindy.

Dear Cindy,

I am totally and utterly and completely fed up. Amanda and her dumb buddies are acting like a bunch of hyperactive chimps next door. Fern has started working a few hours a week in the store and all she can talk about is the best place to put price labels on cans! Pippa has gone kind of loopy and is spending all her time with Andy Melniker! Yes, you read that right. Maybe they're in love or something (yuuuuck!).

So, like I said, I am totally fed up and I wish you were back here. But then I guess you're having a great time, swimming in the ocean every day and stuff like that. It's not fair. It's really not.

I stopped writing. Was I turning into some

kind of total whine-bag or what? That wasn't a letter, it was one long moan. I tore the letter up and dumped the pieces in the wastepaper basket.

Boy, talk about feeling sorry for yourself! If I kept that up, I was due some kind of *award*.

'And now, ladies and gentlemen, it is my proud pleasure to announce the award for The Most Dejected, Depressed, Despondent, Downcast, Gloomy, Heartsick, Miserable, Morose, Sad, Unhappy and Woebegone Person of the Year: the one, the only, the totally fed up and sick to the back teeth – Stacy Allen! Yay!'

(Applause which dies down as I come to the mike.)

'Thank you. Thank you. I'm really unhappy that you should have given me this award. You've made this the most miserable night of my life!'

(More applause as I wave the Statue of Misery in the air and burst into tears.)

I sat up straight at my desk. (I always feel more determined when I sit up straight.) I was going to write Cindy a happy letter. I was going to write her a happy letter if it killed me!

I was going to write a happy letter and I was going to *cheer up*!

There was a big screech of laughter through the wall from Amanda's room.

Well, at least *someone* was enjoying themselves. I just wished it was *me*!

Chapter Five

I knew why the Bimbo Brigade was in Amanda's room that morning making all that noise. They were getting hyped up for some heavy-duty cheerleading that afternoon at a school football game.

Normally I would have gone to cheer our team on, but when Fern had asked me the day before whether I was going, I'd said no, I was busy.

I guess I'd hoped that Fern would say, *Oh, come on, Stacy, it won't be the same without you.* But she hadn't said that at all. She'd said, 'Have you any idea how hard it is to put price tags on bags of frozen peas?'

And now I was sitting in my room, listening to Amanda and her friends getting ready for the game, and knowing that in a couple of hours just about *everybody* would be there. And what would I be busy doing? I'd be busy wishing I hadn't told Fern I was going to be busy!

Anyway, I had that happy letter to write. I took a clean sheet of writing paper from the box Cindy had given me for my tenth birthday.

I suddenly thought that the best way to make the letter *really* happy would be to write it in different coloured inks. I could write every line in a different colour.

I hunted around for some coloured pens. I found three red, a blue and a green that had run out.

Amanda would have coloured pens. She's got heaps of stuff like that for her art projects. For a person with a brain like a peanut, my big sister is the most brilliant artist you could ever meet. I don't know how she does it. I mean, *I* can't draw for beans! Mom can't draw; Dad can't draw – but Amanda is totally brilliant at it.

I knocked on Amanda's door. There was a lot of noise going on in there for only *four* people.

I knocked again and opened the door.

The music was turned up really loud. Cheryl and Rachel were dancing like a couple of crazy people in the middle of the room while Amanda and Natalie yelled and clapped. They were too busy to even notice me.

Cheryl spun Rachel around so they were back to back with their arms linked.

'OK. Go for it!' Cheryl hollered and she doubled up.

'*Nooo! Waiiiit!*' Rachel wailed as she was flipped right over Cheryl's back. Her long skinny legs waved in the air. The next second Cheryl and Rachel were in a heap on the carpet and Amanda and Natalie were splitting with laughter.

Cheryl sat up, her hair looking even more spiky and porcupiney than usual.

'You're supposed to land on your feet!' Cheryl groaned.

'*Urrrrghhhh. Ugggghh. Unnnggggh,*' Rachel moaned.

Cheryl poked her. Right then Rachel looked like a scarecrow that someone had dumped in the middle of the carpet. Her long carrot-red hair was all over her face and her gangly arms and legs were sticking out at strange angles.

I spluttered with laughter.

Four pairs of eyes turned in my direction.

'What do you want, Stacy?' Amanda asked.

'Can I borrow some coloured pens?' I said.

'What for?'

'To write with,' I said, making writing movements in the air. 'I'm writing a letter to Cindy, and I thought it'd look good in different colours.'

'Hey,' Cheryl said. 'Stacy can use real pens

45

now.' She smirked at me. 'Have you used up all your crayons, Stacy?'

'Crayons, *hyuh-hyuh*,' Rachel burbled.

'Yup,' I said. 'I finished up all my crayons a few years ago, Cheryl. How are you managing with your finger-paints?'

Cheryl glared at me. 'I hope you're coming to the game today,' she snarled. 'I've heard that Roseway's mascot died and they're looking for a replacement.' (Roseway Middle School was the team our school was playing.)

'What are you talking about?' I said. 'Roseway's mascot was a goat.'

'Darn right it was!' Cheryl screeched. 'That's why you'd make a perfect replacement!' Rachel and Natalie howled with laughter.

Boy! I'd walked straight into that one!

'Oh, forget it!' I yelled. 'You're just a bunch of brain-dead geeks!' I stormed out and slammed the door.

I marched back to my room.

I sat at my desk and stared out the window, having day-dreams in which all the Bimbos accidentally fell into a bottomless pit of quicksand. I cheered up a little as I imagined Cheryl's spiky hair slowly disappearing under the blooping and blubbing mud.

There was a soft knock on my door and

Amanda came in. Without a word, she walked over to me and placed a tin box in front of me on the desk.

'Coloured pens,' she said.

'*Hmmph!*' I grunted.

'You can borrow them for as long as you like,' Amanda said.

I didn't even look at her.

'In fact,' Amanda said, 'you can keep them.' She tossed her hair. 'I hardly ever use them, anyway.' She pushed the box under my nose. 'Stacy? I'm giving them to you.'

'Yeah, thanks,' I said. 'But goats don't need pens.'

'Aw, Stacy, that was just *Cheryl*. She doesn't mean anything by it. You know what she's like.' She sat on the end of my bed and looked at me without saying anything.

'What?' I said, glaring at her.

'Mom told me you're really missing Cindy.'

'Cindy?' I said. 'Cindy who?'

'Mom said I should be more supportive,' Amanda said. She looked at me. 'She told me you're really upset about Cindy going away.'

'OK,' I said. 'I'm upset. I'm upset and miserable and totally fed up. Are you *happy* now?'

'You shouldn't mope around in here so much,' Amanda said. 'You can come to the game with us if you like.'

47

'I'm not going to the game,' I said.

'Why not?'

'I'm busy.'

'Doing what?' Amanda looked at me. 'Come on, Stacy. Doing *what*, exactly? Staring at the light bulb? Feeling sorry for yourself?' She stood up. 'You know what you need?' she said determinedly. 'You need help, Stacy, before you turn into a complete wimp.'

'I need help?' I said. 'What the heck does that mean?'

Amanda's eyes suddenly lit up. 'I've got it!' she said. 'I know what will make you feel better. A *makeover*! A complete and total makeover. New hair. New face. New clothes. New everything.'

'Oh, gee, fairy godmother,' I said. 'What are you going to do? Wave your magic wand?'

She shook her head. 'Nope,' she said. 'But I'm going to cheer you up if it's the last thing I do.' She reached towards me.

I slid off my chair and backed into the corner. 'You lay one finger on me and it *will* be the last thing you do,' I said. 'I'm warning you, Amanda. You are *not* going to do a make-over on me. I'm perfectly happy the way I look right now.'

Amanda loomed over me with her hands firmly on her hips.

'Now, listen up, Stacy,' she said. 'You're going to be eleven in a week or so. It's about time you started taking an interest in how you look.'

'I like the way I look,' I said.

'But we could make you look so much better,' Amanda said.

'We?' I said. 'Who's *we*? You don't really think I'd let Cheryl and Rachel and Natalie give me a makeover? I'd wind up looking like something from a Halloween party.'

Amanda caught hold of my hand and towed me across the floor.

'Come *on*, Stacy,' she said. 'Everything will be fine. I guarantee it. An hour with Madame Amanda and her high-class makeover squad and you won't recognize yourself.'

'That's what I'm afraid of,' I said as Amanda yanked me along the hall.

But a little voice inside me was saying '*What the heck? You never know, Amanda might be right. Adapt and survive! Go for it!*'

Amanda opened her bedroom door. She put her hands on my shoulders and marched me in ahead of her.

The three Bimbos looked at me.

'Girls,' Amanda said, 'we've got some work to do!'

Chapter Six

'I've changed my mind,' I said as Amanda pulled me inside her room. 'I like the way I look.'

'Oh, no you don't,' Amanda said, closing the door.

'What's the deal?' Cheryl asked.

'We're going to give Stacy a makeover,' Amanda announced.

The three Bimbos grinned. I felt like I'd wandered into a wolf cave.

'What are you going to do to me?' I asked.

'You could do with a whole new look, Stacy,' Amanda said. 'And those clothes have definitely had it!'

I gave Amanda and the Bimbos a suspicious look.

'Give us half an hour,' Amanda said. 'I guarantee you'll look one hundred per cent prettier when we've finished with you.'

I looked at the four faces that surrounded me. To be honest, what did I have to lose?

'OK,' I said, 'make me look fabulous!'

'In half an hour?' Natalie said, plucking at my hair. 'I don't think so.'

'A face-mask would help,' Cheryl said.

'That's it!' I said. 'If you're going to make fun of me, I'm out of here!'

'Stacy! Calm down,' Amanda said. 'Cheryl didn't mean a *Halloween* mask. She meant a skin-toning mask. You put it on your face and it refreshes your skin and makes you feel all healthy and glowy.' She glared at Cheryl. 'That was what you meant, wasn't it?'

'Oh, sure,' Cheryl said with a totally unconvincing smile. 'That's exactly what I meant.'

'OK,' Amanda said. 'Where do we start?'

The four of them closed in on me.

Was this *really* a good idea?

⋆ ⋆ ⋆

I lost track of time. It could have been half an hour, or it could have been two weeks. I was feeling kind of dizzy. I'd been marched to the bathroom to have my hair washed. Cheryl attacked my scalp like she was kneading dough. No one took any notice of me hollering for mercy.

Then I was given a face-mask that was like having green Jell-O smeared all over. I blinked at myself in the mirror. I looked like the

51

ghastly green melting girl from fifty thousand fathoms.

I had hot rollers put in my hair by Natalie while Cheryl and Amanda looked through Amanda's closet in search of some clothes for me to wear. At the same time Rachel gave me a manicure.

'Ow!' I yelled as she filed away at some skin.

'You've got to suffer to be beautiful,' she said as she sawed away at my nails. The way she was going, my nails would wind up filed all the way up to my elbows!

'I think I preferred you guys when we hated each other,' I said, but no one took any notice.

'This might look good,' I heard Amanda say. I turned my head to see what she'd chosen.

'Ow!' I yelped as Natalie nearly pulled out a chunk of my hair.

'So keep still!' Natalie said.

'I don't know,' I heard Cheryl say. 'You don't think it might look a little . . . you know.' I strained an eye around and saw that Amanda was holding up a top.

'A little what?' Amanda said.

'She doesn't have any boobs,' Cheryl hissed.

'We can use tissues,' Amanda said.

'What was that about boobs?' I asked.

'Never you mind,' Amanda said. 'We were talking *about* you, not *to* you.'

'I'm not having tissues stuffed up my front,' I said.

Amanda kind of *glided* over to me, waving her arms in the air.

'If Madame Amanda tells you that tissues down the front are this year's big thing, then you will have tissues down your front, and no arguing. Madame Amanda knows best.'

I washed the green gunge off and Amanda and Cheryl started working on my face.

'I don't want a whole load of make-up,' I said. 'I'm only ten. Mom and Dad would kill me.'

'Shut up,' Amanda said. 'We know what we're doing.'

'But I – *bluurgh*! Yuck!'

'There! I told you to shut up!' Amanda said as I spat out some face-cream that she'd *accidentally* schlooped into my mouth. 'Now keep quiet.'

I kept quiet.

I was pushed and pulled and poked and kneaded and shoved and tweaked and yanked and smeared and blow-dried and filed and stripped to my undies and crammed into new clothes.

'OK!' Amanda said, opening her closet door so I could see myself in her full-length mirror. 'How's *that*!'

I stared at my reflection. It wasn't so much *how's* that as *who's* that?

I stared at myself for a long time. I had shiny, wavy hair. I was wearing one of Amanda's skinny-ribbed tops. I had tissue boobs! I seemed to have fewer freckles than when I'd walked in there and my skin looked kind of *glowy*, just like Amanda had said it would. I was wearing one of Amanda's outgrown skirts, pinned up at the back so it almost looked like it fitted me. I had on a string of fake pearls, and I had clear polish on my fingernails.

I looked *different*. No one could say I didn't look *different*! (Except for my skinny legs poking out from under Amanda's skirt – not even Amanda and her pals could do anything about *them*.)

'Do you like it?' Amanda asked.

'I don't know,' I said slowly.

'Well!' Cheryl snorted. 'Of all the ungrateful – '

'What don't you like about it, Stacy?' Amanda asked. She stood behind me and reached over to adjust my boobs.

'*Those* for a start,' I said.

'I guess they are a little uneven,' Amanda said. 'Hold on a second and I'll prod them into shape.'

'I don't want them prodded into shape,' I said. 'I don't want them *period*!'

'But they look good,' Amanda said.

'Amanda,' I said, 'they look like I have tissues stuffed up my front. One boob is cone-shaped and the other one is kind of squared off.'

'She's right,' Natalie said. 'No one's going to believe she's grown them overnight. Especially not *those* shapes.'

'Fine,' Amanda said. 'Forget the boobs.' She hoiked my boobs out and threw them over her shoulder.

But without my tissue boobs. Amanda's top just hung there on me like a deflated left-over party balloon.

'Try this on instead,' Cheryl said, holding up a dress with a pattern of sunflowers on it. (It was an old one of Amanda's, but I hadn't seen her wear it for ages.) 'I think it'll look better on you.'

I got rid of the top and the skirt and wriggled into the dress. Amanda tied the belt at the back then she did some tucking and straightening and smoothing down.

Cheryl grinned at me. 'What did I say? Does that look great or what?'

I couldn't really believe that it was happening. Wake me up, somebody! Cheryl was being nice to me!

And what was even more amazing was that the dress really did look good. You could see it was just a *little* too big, but not so much that it really mattered.

Amanda got rid of the fake pearls, too.

I took another long look at myself. Did I like it?

Well, you've got to give a person a little while to get used to a new look. I mean, to be honest, right then I just felt kind of *strange*.

'Some nice earrings would set the whole thing off,' Rachel said. 'I know how to pierce ears.' She looked at me. 'I could pierce your ears in no time flat. All I'd need would be a cork and a sterilized needle. I just have to hold the cork against the back of your ear lobe and then go *whack*! right through with the needle. It only takes a second and it doesn't hurt at all.'

'You're kidding?' I said. 'Do I look like I'm insane?'

'No, listen,' Rachel insisted. 'That's how it's done. My cousin Danni had it done for her by a friend.'

'Wait a minute,' Amanda said. 'Didn't your cousin Danni's ear lobes blow up like pumpkins afterwards? And wasn't she rushed to the hospital with blood poisoning?'

'Well, yeah,' Rachel admitted. 'But that was only because the needle wasn't sterilized properly. You have to get rid of all the germs by holding it in a flame for half a minute.'

'Oh, right,' I said. 'So you want to ram a *red-hot* needle through my ears? Why didn't you say so, Rachel? I'd be crazy to refuse an offer like that!'

Rachel blinked at me. 'So, do you want your ears pierced or not?' she said.

'Not!' I said.

'Let's go show Mom,' Amanda said.

'Well, I don't know,' I said. 'Can I *think* about it for a while?' I was nudged across the floor by four pairs of hands and before I knew it I was down in the living room being inspected by Mom and Dad and baby Sam.

'Hey, Amanda,' Dad said, 'Who's your gorgeous new friend?'

'It's me!' I said.

Dad looked amazed. 'It isn't? Is it? It can't be? Can it? Is that glamorous and sophisticated young woman *Stacy*?'

Mom grinned. 'I think it is,' she said. 'You look lovely, sweetheart.'

'We all helped out,' Cheryl said.

'I was in charge of the hair,' Natalie said.

'Well, I'd say you were on course for a career as beauty consultants,' Dad said. 'All of you.' He smiled at me. 'Of course, you won't always have such good material to work with. Stacy is kind of super-gorgeous to begin with.'

'Da-ad!' I said.

'So, Stacy,' Mom said, 'are you going anywhere special with your new look?'

'She's coming to the game with us,' Amanda said. 'Aren't you, Stacy?'

'I guess so,' I said. Well, what was the point of a total makeover if I just sat at home? I might as well find out what people thought of the new me. And maybe then *I* could figure out what I thought of the new me.

'Oh, the *game*,' Dad said. 'You mean the game between your school and Roseway?'

'That's right,' Amanda said.

'The game where you're doing the cheerleading?' Dad said.

'Yes,' Amanda said.

'The game that kicks off in half an hour?' Dad said.

'Wha-a-at???' Amanda spun around and gaped at the wall clock. 'Oh my gosh! Look at the time!'

All four of them started racing around like headless chickens.

'Calm down,' Dad yelled over the noise. 'I'll

drive you there. Just get yourselves out front in five minutes.'

They all went racing up to Amanda's room.

I sat on the arm of the couch. 'Do I really look OK?' I asked Mom.

'You look very pretty, sweetheart,' Mom said. She bounced Sam in her lap. 'Doesn't she, Sam?'

'*Tassy pikky ug!*' Sam said clapping his hands together and giving a gummy grin.

A few minutes later a whole herd of feet came stampeding down the stairs.

'Come on, Stacy!' Amanda yelled.

I joined them out front and we all piled into the car.

Cheryl made some room for me between her and Natalie and we all squeezed in.

'All aboard!' Dad said. 'Wagons ro-oll!'

He drove out into the road and we headed for the sports ground.

'I still think Stacy would look good with pierced ears,' Rachel said.

'Yeah,' I said. 'And you'd look good with a pierced *forehead*!' (It just came out, you know? Force of habit, I guess.)

'A pierced forehead!' Cheryl yelled with laughter. 'I *like* it!'

That was the first time *ever* that Cheryl had laughed at one of my jokes. I could hardly believe what was happening. I hadn't been called a *nerd* for the past hour. I hadn't even been called a *stupid kid* or a *dumb little jerk*. It was almost as if the Bimbos *liked* me all of a sudden.

The *new* me. I grinned as I leaned back in the car. I could see a whole new way of life opening up in front of me. And, hey, maybe Amanda and her friends weren't quite as big airheads as I'd always thought.

Then Amanda started one of their chants: 'Roseway! No way! We are gonna win today!' And then Cheryl and Natalie and Rachel joined in.

By the time Dad dropped us off in front of the school, all five of us were chanting at the tops of our voices.

Wow! Had I cheered up!

Chapter Seven

Luckily the game was running a few minutes late so Amanda and the others just had time to zoom over to join the rest of the squad.

'Stacy!'

I looked around. It was Fern's voice.

'Stacy?'

Fern and Pippa had just come around a corner and were standing staring at me by the entrance to the bleachers. They were wearing FCMS T-shirts and they each had a hot dog in one hand and a can of fizzy drink in the other. (FCMS = Four Corners Middle School.)

'Oh, hi,' I said, feeling kind of embarrassed. (Not just embarrassed because of the way I looked, but embarrassed because I'd told Fern I wouldn't be there.)

Fern came walking towards me with an astonished look on her face and her eyes like saucers. She circled me twice like a suspicious

dog inspecting a new puppy in the neigh-
bourhood.

'You've got curly hair,' Fern said at last. She
came to a halt in front of me. Pippa came over
and stood beside her, her cheeks bulging with
unchewed hot dog.

'I know,' I said.

'*Yob gob gurl grigig og*,' Pippa said through
hot dog.

'Huh?'

Pippa chewed and swallowed. 'You've got
nail polish on.'

'I know,' I said. I waggled my fingers at
them. 'Like it?'

Fern's face came right up close to mine.
'And you've got some kind of face-cream on,'
she said. 'It makes your freckles look paler.'

'Uh-huh,' I said.

'Is that a new dress?' Pippa asked.

For a split second I almost said, *No, it's an
old one of Amanda's*. But what I actually said
was:

'Yeah, I just got it this morning.'

Why did I lie? I guess it was because I
wanted to make them think that the whole
new look was *my* idea. I could tell that they
were impressed. It felt like it might spoil the
effect if I told them that Amanda had been
involved.

Fern took a bite of hot dog. She tilted her head to one side, chewing slowly while she looked me up and down.

'What do you think?' I said.

'I don't like it,' Fern said at last. 'It makes you look dumb. It makes you look like a dumb Amanda clone.'

'It does not!' I said. I was more surprised than angry.

'It does, too,' Fern said. 'And I thought you said you were too busy to come here this afternoon?'

'I thought I was,' I said. 'But in the end I wasn't.' I turned to Pippa. 'Pippa? Do I look like a dumb Amanda clone to you?'

'No,' Pippa said. 'Not a *dumb* one. But your hair is kind of like your sister's. And I'm sure I've seen Amanda in a dress just like that.'

Darn! Pippa had recognized the dress. Why did Pippa have to have such a good memory for stuff like that?

'So, who did the makeover?' Fern asked in a really accusing way.

'I did,' I said.

'Get out of here!' Fern said.

'You didn't let me finish,' I said. 'I was going to say: I did, with some help from . . . from Mom and . . . uh . . . my Aunt Susie.' I really didn't want them to know Amanda had been

63

involved. It was bad enough having them think I was modelling myself on Amanda, without telling them that the whole make-over had been done by her and her pals.

'So, what's it *for*?' Pippa asked.

'What do you mean?' I asked her.

'What made you suddenly decide you wanted to look different?'

'A person's entitled to want to change the way they look,' I said.

'I know,' Pippa said. 'But why *now*? Why today? And why didn't you say anything to us about it?'

'Yeah,' Fern said. 'We could have helped. We could have stopped you from trying to look like a little copy of your sister.'

I was beginning to get annoyed by then. It was like I was on trial or something. Stacy Allen, accused of the terrible crime of wanting to look a little more grown-up. Chief prosecutors: Pippa and Fern.

'For all you two know I could have been talking about it all *week*,' I snapped. I looked at Pippa. 'You've been spending all your time with Andy, for *some* reason,' I said. 'And the only thing Fern's interested in is how much money she's making in her folks' store.'

'And all *you've* been doing is moaning on about how much you miss Cindy!' Fern said.

'It's been "Cindy, Cindy, Cindy" morning, noon and night. And I've got news for you, Stacy: it's *boring*!'

Fern turned and stormed off. I just stood there, totally amazed. I felt like I'd been smacked in the face.

Pippa looked at Fern and then at me, like she couldn't decide whose side she was on.

She gave me a very serious look. 'I know I've been spending a lot of time with Andy recently,' she said. 'There *is* a reason, but I've promised not to tell.'

'Huh?'

Pippa took a deep breath. 'Andy made me promise not to tell anyone,' she said. 'Not yet, anyway.'

'You can tell me.' I said. 'I won't breathe a word.'

'I can't tell you,' Pippa said. 'I'm sorry, but I can't.'

'Well, thanks,' I said. 'Thanks for trusting me, Pippa.'

'Let's not have an argument, Stacy,' Pippa said. 'I hate it when we fight.' She smiled. 'Let's go and find Fern. Then you two can make friends again and we can all watch the game together.'

I looked at her for a few moments.

'OK,' I said. I'd decided that once we'd

found Fern, I'd tell them the truth about the makeover.

'Hey! Stacy!' The call came from behind us. I looked around. The cheerleading squad was racing towards us. It was Amanda who had called. My first thought was to put as much distance between her and me and Pippa as possible.

But I wasn't quick enough.

Amanda put her arm around my shoulders.

'Doesn't she look great?' she said to Pippa. 'You wouldn't believe the fuss she made when I first suggested it.' She grinned at Pippa. 'I practically had to *drag* her into my room, didn't I, guys?'

'Yup,' Cheryl said. 'And it took us over an hour to get her looking this good. And she complained all the way through.'

'Hey,' Amanda said. 'We're going to the Happy Donut after the game. 'Do you want to come with us?'

The Happy Donut was the place where Amanda and her friends hang out. I'd never been invited to go with them before. To be honest, if Amanda had invited me just a couple of weeks ago, I'd have laughed in her face. (Not that she would have invited me a couple of weeks ago.) But I didn't feel like laughing in her face right then. I felt like saying, *I'd* love *to go to the Happy Donut with you.*

'Do you want to come?' I asked Pippa.

'Amanda did the makeover?' Pippa said coldly.

'Well, yes,' I admitted. 'I was going to tell you, but – '

'I'll see you around, Stacy,' Pippa said. '*Maybe.*'

Amanda stared after her.

'What's with her?' she said. 'That kid is so weird sometimes.'

Did I say, *Pippa is not weird, she's my friend*? Did I say, *Pippa is not a kid*?

No. I didn't. I didn't say a single word.

'Come on, you guys,' Natalie said, 'we've got cheerleading to do!'

'Come and sit near us,' Amanda said to me.

So I did. I sat right behind where they did their cheering.

'F! C! M! S! You're the team who are the best! Roseway! No way! You are gonna fry today! Hayyyy-uh! Hayyy-uh! *Yeaaaah!*'

It was really exciting, and by the end of the game everyone was going bananas! We won by fifteen points! It was a total walkover, even though everyone had been saying that Roseway were the best team in the league.

And then I went along with Amanda and the crowd to the Happy Donut.

The place was packed. Every booth was full and the only way I could get a seat was to squeeze myself into a corner seat between Amanda and Rachel. And the place was so *noisy*! Everyone was in a really good mood because of the victory over Roseway.

And when we got home and Mom said, 'Did you have a good time?' I said, 'You bet! I had a *great* time!' And I really meant it, too!

Maybe I'd been wrong about Amanda and her friends. And maybe now that I was *almost* eleven, I was old enough to start being real close friends with Amanda again.

Chapter Eight

I woke up early Sunday morning. My eleventh birthday was only eight days away now. This time next week, my birthday would be *tomorrow*.

I lay in bed for a while, thinking about what presents I might get and going all tingly with anticipation. (I'd been dropping hints about a new bike, but I wasn't sure anyone had noticed.) And then I began to wonder about a party. Mom had said I could invite a few friends over.

Was I still friends with Fern and Pippa? Would they want to come to my party? But how could I throw a party and *not* invite them? Big problem!

Dear Fern, you are hereby invited to the occasion of Stacy's eleventh birthday party. RSVP (That's a fancy way of saying 'Let me know if you're coming'.)

Reply: *Dear Stacy, get lost.*

Benjamin stopped me in mid-think by

jumping up on to the bed and pummelling me with all four paws and *muurping* until I got up and gave him his breakfast.

Once Benjamin was settled I went up to the bathroom for a wash. My new curls were a total mess. It was like I'd been in a typhoon. I tried to comb my hair so that it looked the same as it had yesterday, but it *still* stuck out in clumps all over my head.

I crossed the hallway and knocked softly on Amanda's door. There was no answer. I opened the door and crept into the darkened room.

I could see a big Amanda-lump in the bed.

I gave her a shake.

'Wha'? Wha'? *Stacy!*' Amanda floundered about under the bedcovers. 'What are you *doing*?'

'I can't get my hair to go right,' I explained. 'No matter which way I try to comb it, it keeps going in all the wrong directions.'

Amanda gave me a very expressive look.

Now, to be honest, if I'd thought about it, I'd have remembered that waking Amanda up early on a Sunday morning was not one of the best ideas in the world. Amanda's usual reaction would involve me flying head first out of her window with my neck tied in a knot.

'You're a total pest, do you know that?'

Amanda muttered as she sat up. 'You've got to use a brush, not a comb.' She rubbed the sleep out of her eyes. 'And you've got to go like *that*.' She made a curling kind of motion with her hand. 'You can't just go drag, drag, drag, like before.'

I fetched her brush from her dressing table and she showed me how to kind of *roll* the brush around the curls so they didn't get flattened.

'Do I have to do this every morning?' I asked.

'Yup,' Amanda said, sitting up in bed watching me as I sat at her dressing table and brushed my hair out. 'And every time you wash it, you're going to have to put it in curlers again. That's the problem with having straight hair.' She ran her fingers through her own naturally curly hair. 'Of course,' she said, 'we don't *all* have that problem.'

I looked at her. 'I had a really great time yesterday,' I said.

'Good, that was the plan,' Amanda said with a huge yawn.

I frowned. 'What plan? What do you mean?'

She blinked at me. 'Oh! No plan. Did I say "*plan*"? I don't know why I said "plan". I'm not awake yet, Stacy.' She yawned again and stretched. Then she took a look at her bedside clock. 'Whaaat!' she yelled. 'What kind of time is this? No wonder I'm not awake yet! Stacy, I ought to tie your neck in a knot and dump you out the *window*!'

See what I mean? I was right about how Amanda usually reacted.

I got out of there before she put her ideas into action. A person could have trouble eating her breakfast with a knot in her neck!

* * *

Cindy called around mid-morning and we started off having a really nice chat. I told her about my makeover and she was really impressed. I didn't tell her about how Fern and Pippa had reacted: in fact I hardly mentioned them at all. We spent most of the time talking about my birthday and remembering previous birthdays and having a good laugh about it.

'I'm going to send your present to you,' Cindy told me.

'What is it? What is it?' I asked.

'It's a secret.'

'What kind of secret?'

'A *secret* kind of secret,' Cindy said. 'If I told you it'd spoil the surprise.'

'Oh, go on, Cindy. Tell me!'

'OK, I'll tell you if you really want me to.'

'Noooo! Don't tell me. Just give me a clue. Is it heavy or light?'

'Yes.'

'Cindy!'

'Well, some people might think it was heavy, and some people might think it was light,' Cindy said, really helpfully.

'What size is it?'

'About *so* long,' Cindy said, 'and about *this* high.'

I snorted down the phone. 'What kind of a clue is *that*?'

She laughed. 'You'll just have to wait,' she said. 'Are you having a party?'

'I guess,' I said. 'I haven't really thought about it.'

'But it's next week,' Cindy said. 'Shouldn't you have it all planned by now?'

She was right, of course. But I managed to change the subject and she spent most of the rest of the call telling me about San Diego and about her new school and a girl she sat next to called Shannon. It sounded to me like she and Shannon were spending a lot of time together.

'She's nice,' Cindy told me. 'We get along really well.'

'Great,' I said. But I didn't really mean it. I just got so jealous of this *Shannon*. Who did she think she was, muscling in on my best friend?

I felt kind of gloomy after the call.

Later on I was sitting on my bed when the door flew open and Amanda came in. (Amanda isn't the kind of person who knocks – she says knocking's for wimps.)

'Hey, I could have been changing!' I said.

'Into what? A frog?' Amanda said. She came and sat on the bed next to me. 'About this party of yours.'

I gazed at her. 'What party?'

'Your *birthday* party, dumbo,' Amanda said. 'Remember? You're going to be eleven next week. People have parties to celebrate their birthdays. It's what people do.' She grinned at me. 'Because it's *fun*.'

'Yeah,' I said. 'So?'

'So what plans have you made?'

'None, so far,' I said.

'Fine!' Amanda said. 'That's just what I wanted to hear.'

I gave her a puzzled look. 'Why?'

'Well, picture this,' Amanda said. 'Scene one: a dull, boring kind of party with a few packs of potato chips, one tub of Thousand Island dip, a single carton of grape juice and a whole load of totally boring people.'

'Amanda, I – '

'Shh! Now picture *this* scene: Party decorations. A whole table full of food and drink. Some brilliant *loud* music and the whole house buzzing with really interesting and fun people.' She put her fist under my nose as if she was clutching a microphone. 'Now, then, Stacy Allen, of Four Corners, Indiana, this is your sixty-four-thousand dollar question. Which kind of party sounds more fun to you? Think carefully, now. Party A – the *boring* party. That's a little clue for you, Stacy. The *BORING* party. Or party B – the exciting and brilliant and fun party.'

'Well, Amanda,' I said, acting like a game-show contestant. 'I'm not too sure about this, but . . . uh . . . I think I'll go for the . . . uh . . . the *fun* party.'

Amanda jumped up and pranced around like a genuine game-show host. 'That's the correct answer!' she yelled.

'Amanda,' I said, 'what are you doing?'

'I am going to plan your entire party, Stacy. You won't have to lift a finger. I'll send out the invitations. I'll put up the decorations. I'll make sure there's heaps of food and stuff. I'll make up some tapes of the best party music you've ever heard.' Amanda beamed at me and spread her arms out. 'I'll do *everything*!' she said. 'It'll be my present to you. A mega-brilli-ant party! What do you say?'

I stared at her with my mouth open.

She put her hands on her hips. 'You say, "Thank you, Amanda, you are truly the most wonderful and caring and loving sister in all the world." *That's* what you say.'

I gazed up at her. I had the feeling like I was about to step on board a total monster of a white-knuckle ride.

'Thank you, Amanda,' I said. 'You are truly the most wonderful and caring sister in the world.'

'Right on!' Amanda said. 'You missed out "loving", but I forgive you.'

'Amanda, what exactly are you – '

'Can't stop!' Amanda said as she sprinted for the door. 'Too busy! Party to organize! Things to do! People to see! Catch you later!'

All Points Weather Alert! Hurricane Amanda heading for Four Corners. Tie down all your valuables! Make for the storm cellar! Women, children and cats first!

What exactly *had* I let myself in for?

Chapter Nine

I could hear Mom and Amanda talking in the kitchen as I went downstairs for breakfast the following morning.

'How am I doing?' Amanda was asking.

'You're doing just fine,' Mom said. 'I'm sure you're helping her a lot, honey. I'm really proud of you.'

'Hi, everyone,' I said as I went into the kitchen. I looked at Amanda. 'What are you doing?'

'I'm eating breakfast,' Amanda said. She was at the table with a bowl of cereal.

'I can see *that*,' I said. 'I meant what are you doing that Mom's proud of?'

'Maybe Mom's just proud of the way I eat breakfast,' Amanda said. She looked over to where Sam was sitting in his highchair splashing oatmeal all over. 'I do it a whole lot better than *some* people around here.'

'You leave Sam out of it,' Mom said. 'He's

doing very well. I'd like to see how you got on if you had to do everything in boxing gloves.'

'What's boxing gloves got to do with anything?' Amanda asked. 'He's not wearing boxing gloves.'

'At Sam's age,' Mom explained, 'the control you've got in your hands is about the same as an adult wearing boxing gloves.'

'Is that true?' I said, watching Sam with new admiration.

Dad came racing into the kitchen in his coat. He whipped the spoon out of Amanda's hand and scooped up some cereal. Still chewing, he kissed Amanda and Sam goodbye. He opened his briefcase and Mom dropped his lunch into it. He kissed Mom, kissed me and was out of there in about fifteen seconds flat.

'Whoops!' we heard from the hall and he came running back in to give Amanda her spoon back.

The front door banged and he was gone.

'Bye, honey,' Mom said to the empty doorway. 'Have a nice day.'

I ate breakfast and a few minutes later I was waiting with Amanda at the bus-stop.

'Have you thought any more about my party?' I asked.

'I sure have,' Amanda said. 'I'm going to the mall this afternoon to pick up some invitations and some decorations and stuff like that. I think we should invite thirty people.'

'*Thirty?*' I said. 'I don't *know* thirty people. We'll never fit thirty people into the house. Mom won't let me have thirty people, no way.'

'Mom's cool about it,' Amanda said. 'Anyway, not all of them will be able to come. You always invite *more* than you want because a few people always drop out. My guess is that we'll wind up with between twenty and twenty-five guests.'

'That's just about everyone in my class,' I said. 'I'm not sure I want to invite *all* of them. I'd rather just have around ten people, if it's all the same to you.'

Amanda's hands went on to her hips.

'Stacy, if someone offers to organize the greatest party that Four Corners has ever seen as a birthday present for you, then I think you should act like you're grateful, rather than constantly criticizing what a person is doing.'

'Sorr-ee,' I said. 'I won't say another word, I promise.'

'Good. I hope *not.*'

'Uh, except – '

'*Grr!*'

'I just want to make sure you don't invite the wrong people,' I said. 'Like, I don't much

79

want Betsy-Jane Garside to be invited, because I can't stand her.'

'Stacy, trust me to pick a good crowd of people,' Amanda said.

'You can send an invitation to Denise di Novi,' I said. 'She's OK. And Larry Franco, he's OK, too. But not Sophie Carpenter.'

'Listen, Stacy,' Amanda said. 'I'll be honest with you. I wasn't planning on inviting any of those people.'

'You weren't?'

'They're *kids*,' Amanda said. 'Do you really want a bunch of kids at your eleventh birthday party, Stacy? Now that you're going to be eleven, it's time you started hanging out with some older people. If you hang around with kids, Stacy, you're going to keep on acting like a kid yourself. But if you make some friends that are a little older than you, then you'll start behaving like them. Do you see what I'm getting at?'

'I guess so,' I said. 'But what sort of older people are you talking about?'

'People my age,' Amanda said.

'You mean your friends?'

'That's right.'

'So, let me see if I understand what's going on here,' I said. 'It's my party, but you're inviting *your* friends. You're not planning on inviting any of *my* friends at all?'

'It's for your own good,' Amanda insisted. 'My friends are all really fun. You'll have a great time. I've already talked to Cheryl and Natalie and Rachel about it and they're all really looking forward to it.'

'I bet they are.'

Amanda glared at me. 'Oh, I get it,' she said. 'You think I'm doing all this for my own benefit. You think I'm inviting my friends so that *I* can have a good time. Well, thanks very much for the vote of confidence, Stacy. If I wanted to have a party, then I'd *have* a party. But I wanted it to be *your* party, Stacy. I wanted you to join in. I wanted you to enjoy yourself.'

'OK!' I said. 'Don't blow a fuse. I'm sorry. Really. It's totally terrific of you to organize my party, and I'm really grateful. I'm just not sure what to do if anyone in my class asks what I'm doing for my birthday. What if they ask if I'm having a party? What do I say?'

'Tell them there isn't going to be one.' Amanda said without batting an eyelid. 'Anyway, who's going to ask?'

'Pippa, for one,' I said. 'And Fern. I can't not invite *them*, Amanda. They're my best friends. At least, they *were*, and I'm sure they

81

will be again, once we start talking to each other. But if I have a party without them they'll never speak to me again for the rest of my life.'

'Big loss!' Amanda mumbled.

'Amanda!'

'OK, OK. Leave it to me. I'll invite Fern and Pippa, if you really want me to. But no one else from your class, OK? This is going to be a high-class, exclusive, sophisticated and totally *grown-up* party, got me?'

'Got you,' I said.

The bus came trundling around the corner.

'Oh, one little thing,' Amanda said. 'There's no need for you to talk to Fern and Pippa about the party – leave all that to me, OK?'

'Yeah, sure,' I said.

I saw Fern sitting with Paula Byrne from our class.

Good, I thought, *that saves me from having to decide whether to sit with Fern or to avoid her.*

* * *

It is so strange the way things break up. A month ago Cindy and Fern and Pippa and I did just about *everything* together. We all sat together in class. We sat at the same table in the cafeteria. We hung around together and spent time at each other's houses.

And four weeks later, Cindy was in California with her new friend *Shannon*, and I wasn't even talking to Pippa and Fern. And not only *that*, but it looked like I was turning into an honorary member of the Bimbo Brigade!

We always used to call Amanda and her friends the Bimbo Brigade and they'd call us the Nerds. I figured I'd better stop thinking of Cheryl and the others as Bimbos now. Now that it looked like they were going to be my friends.

★   ★   ★

It was lunchtime. I picked up my tray from the counter and looked across the cafeteria to our usual table. I couldn't believe my eyes! Fern was there already, and so was Pippa. And do you want to take a guess at who *else* was sitting there? Sitting in *my* place?

Andy Melniker, that's who!

Well, I didn't need a neon sign flashing *Stacy, Go Away!* to figure out that I wasn't wanted!

I looked around and saw Amanda and her pals sitting together at another table. I'd show Pippa and Fern just how much I cared about *them*!

I made my way over to Amanda's table.

'Hi, guys,' I said. 'Is there room for me?'

Cheryl gave me a sour kind of look.

'Sure,' she said. 'Barge right in, why don't you. *Owww!*' She grabbed her shin with both hands.

'Sorry, Cheryl,' Amanda said sweetly, 'did I accidentally kick you?' She looked up at me. 'Hi, Stacy. Sit down.'

I sat down. I gave Cheryl a puzzled look. For a moment there she'd behaved like the old *Stacy-hating* Cheryl.

But now she forced a smile as she rubbed frantically at her shin. 'How's things, Stacy?' she said between her teeth.

'OK,' I said as I edged my tray in among theirs.

Suddenly Rachel burst out laughing for no reason.

'I'm sorry,' she giggled with her hands over her mouth. 'I can't help it.'

'What's so funny?' I asked.

'Nothing!' Amanda snapped, glaring daggers at Rachel. 'Just some dumb joke she was telling us.'

'Go on then,' I said. 'Tell me.'

Rachel's face went blank.

'Tell Stacy the joke, Rachel,' Amanda said.

'Uh,' Rachel's face went even blanker. 'Oh, yeah!' she said after a few seconds. 'How many teachers does it take to change a lightbulb?'

84

'I don't know,' I said. 'How many?'

'Beats me,' Rachel said. 'I was home sick that day.'

I looked at her. 'You were laughing at *that*?' I said. 'That joke is so weak it should be on life support!'

'Life support!' Cheryl laughed. 'Nice one, Stacy!'

'So,' Natalie said, smiling at me. 'What's new, Stacy?'

There was something I wanted to talk about, although I had the feeling that Amanda's friends weren't going to find it very interesting.

'Well,' I said. 'Did any of you see that really good programme on television yesterday? It was all about time travel. You know, if it's possible for people to travel backwards and forwards through time. Most of the people on the programme said it was totally impossible, but there was this one guy who – '

'Speaking of TV,' Cheryl interrupted. 'Did anyone see that interview with Cal Hooper on MTV? Was his hairstyle dumb or *what*? That guy has just gone completely downhill recently.'

'It's all the fault of that total bimbo of a girlfriend he has,' Natalie said. 'Lola Schwartz! *Blecch!* Did you know, she's had, like, seven separate operations on her body to get her to that shape?'

'Yeah,' Rachel said. 'I read she had three operations just on her nose.'

'And it still looks like a ski slope!' Amanda said and they all laughed.

'Anyway,' I said. 'This one guy – he was some kind of professor or something – he said that time travel *was* possible. And I was thinking, wouldn't it be amazing if we *could* go back in time? Guys? Wouldn't it?'

'There is no way on *earth* that I would do that,' Cheryl said.

'Why not?' I asked. 'I'd love to. It'd be brilliant.'

'You've got to be kidding!' Cheryl said, pulling an appalled face. 'No one is gonna lie me on a table and suck two pints of fat out of my butt!'

'Is that what they do?' Rachel asked.

'Uh-huh.' Cheryl nodded. 'They shove this thing like a vacuum cleaner hose in through your skin. And then they switch it on, and you can see all the fat draining into this big tank. It's totally gross! And you're like, totally bruised to bits for weeks afterwards.'

'I was talking about time travel!' I said. 'Not plastic surgery. If I could go back in time, I'd like to – '

'And sometimes it goes wrong!' Natalie said as if I wasn't even speaking. 'And you wind up with a face like a mangled-up pizza! I read about this woman who had her eyelids fixed by some total jerk of a doctor. And she hasn't been able to close her eyes since the operation! Not even to blink! She has to have special eye drops to stop her eyes from drying up and falling out!'

All the rest of them wriggled around on their chairs and made disgusted squirming noises.

'Yeah, but that hardly ever happens,' Amanda said. 'Mostly it works really well. When I get old and wrinkly, I'm sure going to have some work done on me. No way am I going to wind up looking like an old lady. I'm going to stay young and beautiful for ever.'

'Huh,' Cheryl said. 'If you can afford it!'

'Sure I'll be able to afford it,' Amanda said. 'I'm gonna marry Eddie Eden. He can pay for it all!'

'Eddie Eden wouldn't marry you!' Natalie said. 'You're too young. He might *adopt* you I guess.'

'Older men marry beautiful young women all the time,' Amanda said.

And then they all started blabbing on about who they all wanted to marry and where they'd want to live and what colour limousine they'd want and stupid stuff like that.

I didn't manage to get another *word* in about anything else. I glanced over to where Fern, Pippa and Andy were sitting. I bet they were talking about something more interesting than getting rich and living in a mansion.

I was beginning to wonder if being friends with Amanda and her gang was going to be so much fun after all. I mean, there's only so much brainless blabbing a sane person can put up with. And one lunchtime with Cheryl and the rest was just about my limit!

Chapter Ten

A couple of afternoons later I was sitting on the wall outside school waiting for Amanda.

I didn't usually go home with Amanda. Normally I'd have gone home with Cindy or Pippa or Fern, or at least I'd have spent some time talking to them after school. But things were different now. I hadn't spoken a single word to Pippa or Fern for *days*. And they hadn't spoken to me either.

While I waited for Amanda I had time for a good *think* about the situation I was in.

All this week I had spent my lunchtimes with Amanda and Co. But they never wanted to talk about anything I found interesting. Sure, they were still being nice to me, but most of the time I just sat there with my mouth shut, staring out of the window while they blabbed on about boys and clothes and what shade of lipstick looked best on them.

I felt like saying, *Who cares what lipstick you wear, Cheryl? Your mouth is always moving so fast that no one would ever get to see it! It'd just be a blur!*

And Rachel was constantly telling dumb stories that didn't make any sense because she'd always get everything in the wrong order.

'So I'm, like, standing in the shoe store, waiting for the assistant to come back. Oh, no, it wasn't the shoe store at all! I remember. That was a totally different time. The assistant had gone off with my shoe and she'd, like, totally forgotten about me and gone to lunch. But that wasn't it. I was in some other store. I don't remember which one. And I saw that *girl*. You know, the one from Roseway? You know who I mean! The one that went out with that boy with all the zits? No, wait! It wasn't him. It was his *friend* she went out with. We saw them at the movies that time when Natalie was talking to that ugly-looking kid in the burger bar. You remember?' And on and on until I felt like sticking my fingers in my ears and *screaming*!

And Natalie only had one subject that interested her. And that subject was *Natalie*. Natalie's hair. Natalie's fingernails. Natalie's clothes. Natalie's bathtime routine. Natalie could talk about Natalie for *hours*.

I had a real problem. I wanted to be friends with Amanda like we were when we were younger. But Amanda and her friends were driving me nuts with boredom! If *this* was being grown-up, then I'd rather stay *ten* for the rest of my life.

I was sitting on the wall, thinking about all that stuff, when I heard a familiar voice behind me.

' "Humpty Dumpty sat on a wall," ' Fern said. 'And we all know what happened to Humpty Dumpty. Humpty Dumpty had a *big* fall.'

I looked round. Fern glared at me, but Pippa looked more unhappy than angry.

'Tell *Fern*,' I said to Pippa, 'that she's about as funny as a rock.'

'And tell Stacy,' Fern said to Pippa, 'that the bigger people's heads get, the more their tiny brains rattle around inside!'

'And you can just about darned well ask Fern what she means by that!' I said to Pippa. 'If she means anything. Which I doubt!'

'Tell Stacy,' Fern said to Pippa, 'that if she hadn't gotten so dumb recently, she'd *know* what I was talking about. I'm talking about her being too snooty for us these days. I'm talking about her spending all her time with the *big* girls. *Big* girls, teeny-weeny *brains*. And tell her that if a person spends too much time

91

with a bunch of airhead Bimbos, then she'll wind up a Bimbo herself! Tell her *that*!'

'And tell Fern,' I yelled at Pippa, really angrily, 'that if I cared twice as much as I *do* about her opinion, then I'd still care half as much as she deserves! So *there*!'

'Tell her *what*?' Pippa said.

Fern looked at me. 'What did you just say?' she asked me.

'I don't *know*!' I hollered. 'And I don't care!'

'Wait a minute,' Pippa said. 'I think I know what Stacy meant. She meant to say that if she cared *half* as much as she does about your opinion, then she'd still care *twice* as much as you deserve.' Pippa looked up at me. 'Wasn't that it?'

I folded my arms really huffily. 'That's exactly what I said!'

'No it wasn't,' Fern said. 'You said it the other way around.'

'Oh, shut up,' I said. 'I'm not talking to you!'

'Well, that's just fine with me!' Fern yelled. 'Cos I'm not talking to you!'

'Well, I'm not talking to you a whole lot more than you're not talking to me!' I shouted. 'I'm not going to talk to you again if I live for a hundred years!'

'I'm not going to talk to you again if I live for a *thousand* years!' Fern yelled.

'That's just stupid,' I said. 'No one lives for a thousand years!'

'That's all you know!' Fern said. 'I saw a TV programme last weekend about time travel. And one guy said he thought people would be able to travel through time one day. And if that happened, then I'd be able to go a thousand years into the future, right? And if I *did*, I still wouldn't talk to you!'

'You said you wouldn't talk to me if you *lived* for a thousand years,' I said. 'If you travel a thousand years into the future, you'll still be the same age as you were when you left. You wouldn't be a thousand years old!'

'Yes, I would!'

'No, you wouldn't! Pippa! Tell her!'

'My mom says time travel contravenes all known laws of physics,' Pippa said. 'So there's no point in even talking about it.'

'She says it does *what* with all known laws of which?' Fern asked.

'Contravenes the laws of physics,' Pippa said. 'It means doing something that doesn't make any kind of sense.'

'Huh!' I said. 'That's all your mom knows! I bet there *will* be time travel!'

'Yeah, me too,' Fern said.

'Well, if there *is*,' Pippa said, 'then the first thing you two need to do is to go back in time to before you stopped talking to each other, cos I'm totally sick of us not being friends any more.'

'Oh, yeah?' I said, glaring at Fern. 'And whose fault is that? Who told me I was being boring?'

'Excuse me,' Fern snapped, 'but I seem to remember someone telling me I was being boring before I told them *they* were being boring.'

'Well, you were,' I said.

'I was what?' Fern said.

'Being boring,' I said.

'Hey, guys!' Pippa said. 'Quit arguing!'

'I was not being boring!' Fern yelled.

'You were, too!' I yelled back. I looked at Pippa. 'And I'm not arguing. Fern is the one who's arguing!'

'You can tell Stacy that *she* started it!' Fern said to Pippa.

'Tell her I did not!' I told Pippa.

'You're both driving me crazy!' Pippa hollered at the top of her voice. 'I'm getting out of here before I lose my mind!'

Pippa stormed off in one direction. Fern marched off in another direction. And I sat on the wall, as mad at Fern as the maddest person in the world had ever been mad at anyone. Maybe even a little bit more!

Chapter Eleven

Over the final couple of days before the big party I tried to find out exactly what Amanda was planning.

'Amanda,' I said on Thursday, 'what sort of food are we having?'

Amanda said, 'Leave it to me, Stacy. It's under control.'

And I said, 'Amanda, I'd like to help you pick what goes on the music tapes, if that's OK.'

And she said, 'We've already made the tapes. Cheryl and I did it last night.'

On Friday I asked, 'How many people are coming?'

'Twenty-two for sure,' Amanda said.

'Does that leave room for me to invite a couple more of *my* friends besides Pippa and Fern?' I asked.

'I thought we agreed about this party,' Amanda said. 'No nerdy kids.'

I didn't say another word. I mean, how

could I possibly tell Amanda that I was getting really annoyed at the way she'd taken over my party? How do you say to a person, *Excuse me. Thanks for all the work you've put in, but I've decided I want to run my party MY way, I want MY friends there. I want MY kind of music. In fact, Amanda – and I hope you don't take this the wrong way – but I WANT MY BIRTHDAY PARTY BACK*!

Would Amanda say:

A) 'Gee, thanks, Stacy. I wanted out, to be honest, but I didn't want to let you down.'

B) 'Stacy, that's really good news! I'm sure you'll do a much better job with it that I ever could.'

C) 'Stacy, I've worked my rear end off for you and *this* is all the thanks I get! I hate you more than words could possibly tell! You are no longer my sister! I *have* no sister! I am an only child! Uh, except for Sam.

D) '*Arrrrrrrrrgggggghhhhh!* Kill Stacy! Kill Stacy! Kill! Kill! KILL!!!'

I think the smart money would be on either C or D.

* * *

It was Saturday morning. I was lying in bed with Benjamin on top of me, *murrping* and demanding attention.

It was the day of my birthday party. So why wasn't I feeling excited? How come I was lying there thinking the whole thing had been a big mistake?

I could picture the scene in school on Monday.

'Hey, Stacy, isn't it your birthday today? Are you having a party?'

'Uh, yeah.'

'Great! When?'

'Last Saturday. Don't get offended, but you weren't invited because you're a bunch of nerdy little kids. We can still be friends, though, huh? Hey, guys! Calm down! What did I say?

Yeah, right! When news of my *grown-up* party hit my class, I'd be about as popular as a bad smell in a spacesuit!

I sat up. I tipped Benjamin on to his back and stroked his tummy. He lay there for a while with all four legs in the air.

I got out of bed. Benjamin sat there looking annoyed with me, like he does whenever I stop petting him.

'Sorry, Benjamin,' I said. 'I'll give you a good brushing later.'

I headed off to the bathroom. I could hear Amanda's voice coming up the stairs. I leaned over the banister rail. She was sitting on the stairs and gabbing on the phone.

'Of course she doesn't mind,' Amanda was saying. 'She'll have a great time.' She caught sight of me and waved. She pointed to the phone and mouthed 'Party business' to me and gave me a thumbs up.

I came out of the bathroom and sat on the top stair waiting for Amanda to finish her call.

'Who was that?' I asked as she put the receiver down.

'Matt Clarke,' she said.

'Who?'

'Oh, you know him. He's the brother of the girl who was sitting next to Tony Scarfoni in the Happy Donut last Saturday.'

'What girl?' I said. 'The girl with the red ribbons in her hair and the weird laugh?'

'No, you're thinking of Caroline Nance. Pamela Clarke was the one in the green velvet top. With the stud in her nose.'

'I don't remember her,' I said. 'I don't remember her at all.'

'No big deal, you'll see her soon anyway,' Amanda said with a shrug. 'They're all great people. You'll like them. Matt is really funny.'

'Amanda,' I said determinedly, 'exactly how many of the people who are coming to my party do I know?'

She laughed. 'You know me, for a start,' she said. 'And you know James, and Rachel, and Cheryl.' She reeled off about a dozen names of classmates of hers.

'But that's only about *half* the number you said were coming,' I said. 'So my party is going to be half-full of people I don't even know!'

'That's the whole point of parties,' Amanda said cheerfully. 'To meet new people.'

'I'd really like to invite some of my friends,' I said.

Amanda stared at me. 'Huh?'

'I want to invite some people from my class,' I said. 'I know Pippa and Fern are coming, but there are at least ten other people who will be really upset if they aren't invited.'

Amanda threw her arms in the air. 'Well, fine!' she said. 'I've worked by backside off for you all week, Stacy. I've planned everything down to the last detail to try and make this a really fabulous party for you. But if you want to go and ruin everything at the last minute, then fine.' She came storming up the stairs past me. 'Just wait there and I'll give you the list of all the people I invited. You can spend the morning calling and telling them they can't come because you've decided you want a kiddies' party after all.'

Dad came out of the living room.

'What's all the shouting about?' he asked.

'Nothing important!' Amanda hollered over the banisters. 'Just Stacy throwing my birthday present back in my face!'

She slammed into her bedroom.

Dad frowned up at me.

'No problem,' I said to him. 'It was a tiny misunderstanding, that's all. I'll sort it out.'

I knocked on Amanda's door.

'Go away!'

I went in. She was sitting on a beanbag cushion on the floor, pretending to read a magazine.

'Look,' I said.

She glared at me. 'I'm looking,' she said.

'Amanda, listen.'

'I'm listening, too,' she said. 'I'm all eyes and ears, Stacy. What do you want now? Do you want me to go to the movies while you have your party? After all, you don't want any older people there. They might ruin it for you!'

I sat on the edge of her bed. 'Don't be like that,' I said. 'I'm really, truly grateful for all the work you've put in. Honest, I am. But what if my friends find out I had a party and I didn't invite them? They'll be really annoyed at me. Half of my class probably won't ever talk to me again.'

'Well,' Amanda said, 'if that's the problem,

why don't you have a small sleepover party next week for your school friends?'

'They probably won't want to come,' I said. 'They'll all hate me because they didn't get invited today.'

'Well,' Amanda said, 'if they're going to behave like such little kiddies, then you're better off without them. Face it, Stacy, you're the first one of your friends to hit eleven. And eleven is different from ten.'

'Yeah,' I said. 'When I was ten I had a whole bunch of friends. When I'm eleven I won't have *any*.'

'Correction,' Amanda said. 'You'll have a whole gang of new friends.'

I heard Dad calling up the stairs.

'Are you ready to go to the mall, Stacy?'

Oh, yeah! I'd almost forgotten. Dad was going to take me shopping with the early birthday money I had from my grandparents.

I ran to get dressed. There would be time to finish the party talk with Amanda when I got back. Just then I had other things to think about. I had Grandma and Grandpa's birthday money to think about.

In less than ten minutes I was in the car with Dad and we were heading for the mall. And I wasn't going to leave there until I'd done some serious shopping!

Chapter Twelve

'I thought you were never going to make your mind up!' Dad said as we drove home. 'I was about to call your mom and ask her to bring out a couple of folding beds and a thermos of coffee.'

'It's not *easy* spending birthday money,' I tried to explain. 'There were lots of different things that I really liked. I had to decide whether I wanted to spend all my money on one thing, or whether I wanted to buy lots of things that cost less, see? I could have bought that book on nature reserves, plus those bangles and the T-shirt with the dolphin on it.'

'So what helped you decide?' Dad asked as we drove along.

'Well,' I said, 'the way I look at it, I can buy all *those* things separately some other time when I've got less money. Which is why I bought the shoes.'

I was clutching a bag with *Footloose Freddie Frobisher – Purveyor of Perfect Pedal Apparel* printed on it. (The *Purveyor of* . . . stuff means he sells shoes.) I'd been drooling over a really neat pair of shoes on display in the window for the last few weeks.

The only problem had been that they cost more than Grandad and Grandma's money. So I had to put Plan 414 into action.

Plan 414. Note: this plan only works on Dad. Do not attempt this plan on Mom, she is *wise* to it! (It's called 414 because D is the fourth letter of the alphabet and A is the first. Get it?)

Choose an item in a store window which you cannot afford. Gaze longingly at it and sigh a lot. Possibly say, '*If I had just one wish in the whole wide world, then I'd wish I had enough money to buy* . . . (insert your desired item here) . . . *but I don't, so I guess I'll just have to save and save until I can afford it.*'

Go away from the window and do other things, but always return to the store and repeat the gazing and sighing business as often as necessary.

Dad can't hold out against that kind of thing for more than ten minutes. He gave me the rest of the money and I zipped into Footloose Freddie's to buy the shoes.

We got home and I showed Mom what I had bought.

'She can wrap you around her little finger,' Mom said to Dad as I paraded around the living room in my new shoes. 'I know *exactly* how much they cost, and I told her she'd have to save up for them.'

'She's going to pay me back out of her allowance,' Dad said, giving me a wink.

'That'll be the day,' Mom said.

There were yells and clatters from the kitchen.

'That's Amanda and Cheryl and Natalie,' Mom said in a gloomy voice. 'I've been banished while they get the party ready.' She looked at Dad. 'And we've been given strict instructions to keep a low profile during the party.'

'I think I'll go and visit Bob,' Dad said. (Bob is a pal of Dad's. He lives a few streets away.)

'Oh, thanks,' Mom said. 'Leave me to deal with any trouble.'

'Stacy's friends are never any trouble,' Dad said.

'OK,' Mom said. 'You can hide out at Bob's. But you're taking Sam with you.'

The doorbell rang. It was Rachel. She came in dragging half a dozen filled shopping bags with her.

Amanda appeared.

'OK,' she said to me. 'Upstairs!'

'Why?' I asked.

'We've got to get you ready,' she said. 'You can't go to your own party looking like . . . like – *that*!'

'Don't get carried away,' Mom called as Amanda led me up the stairs. 'I don't want her coming back down looking like a painted doll!'

'Can't I wear just a little make-up?' I asked.

'A *very* little,' Mom said firmly. 'Amanda? Are you listening?'

'Yes, Mom,' Amanda called down as we went into the bathroom for stage one of getting me ready for the party.

* * *

Amanda was in a really good mood and we were joking and laughing all the way through washing and curling my hair and choosing something special for me to wear.

'What about the sunflower dress again?' Amanda asked.

'No, I don't think so,' I said. I remembered that Pippa had recognized it. I wanted to wear something that didn't make me look like a little Amanda clone.

I picked a yellow dress of mine.

Amanda examined me with her chin in her hand. 'Too *little-girlie*,' she said.

I went and picked out a blouse and skirt.

'Too *formal*,' Amanda announced. I marched back to my room and slung on an old pair of jeans.

'Too *scruffy*!'

'Amanda! I'm running out of choices.'

Cheryl came up to help choose.

'I still think the sunflower dress is the nicest,' Cheryl said. She looked at Amanda. 'I've got to go to the store for a couple of things. Coming?'

'Sure,' Amanda said. 'Stacy,' she said to me as she followed Cheryl out, 'it's the sunflower dress or *nothing*.'

'Ugh! Not *nothing*!' I heard Cheryl say as they went down the stairs. 'Everyone will think a pink stick insect has escaped from the zoo!'

'Shh! She'll hear you!' I heard Amanda say. 'You *promised*!'

I ran to the door to listen as their voices got fainter.

'I'm doing my best,' Cheryl said. And then the front door closed behind them.

There was something going on between those two. What did Amanda mean by '*You promised*'? What had Cheryl promised? And what did Cheryl mean when she said she was doing her best?

'Well,' Mom said, coming out of her bedroom. 'Let's have a look at you.'

'Amanda only put a little bit of make-up on me,' I said.

'Uh-huh?' Mom said looking me up and down. 'Well,' she said with a smile, 'you're gorgeous.'

'Am I?'

'Totally. Oh, by the way. did Amanda give you the message?'

'What message?'

'I don't know. There was a call for you while you were out. Amanda answered it. I heard her say, "OK, I'll tell her." Didn't she say anything to you?'

'Nope,' I said. 'I'll ask her when she gets back.'

Except that I didn't get the chance when Amanda got back. Natalie came up and insisted that I had to stay in my room until everything was ready downstairs.

I could hear a lot of activity down there. The doorbell rang and I heard James's voice.

'Hi, James!' I yelled down the stairs. 'I'm not allowed down.'

James came up to talk to me for a while. I get along really well with James. He told me

I looked *glamorous*. He teased me a little by saying I could easily pass for eighteen.

Yeah, right! I'm totally the wrong shape for eighteen. Unless he meant an eighteen-year-old beanpole.

The doorbell started ringing and I could hear people arriving, and Amanda still wouldn't let me downstairs.

I was beginning to think that the only way I was ever going to get to attend my own party was if I shimmied down the drainpipe and rang the front doorbell!

Then Amanda came up and said everything was ready for my *grand entrance*.

For a couple of seconds I felt kind of nervous. But I did one of my mom's anti-nervousness tricks. (Take your nervousness and put it in a box. Put a lid on the box and tie it up with string. Then put the box in a drawer in a cabinet and lock the drawer. Leave the room and lock the door behind you. And, if you're feeling extra-special nervous, you can go right out of the house and catch a train to another part of the country! Yeah, I know it sounds kind of silly, but it really works.)

I went downstairs. The living room was decorated all over with paper chains and streamers and balloons, and there was a big *HAPPY BIRTHDAY* banner on one wall. And the room was full of people. And as I walked in they all began to sing, 'Happy birthday to you, happy birthday to you, happy bi-i-i-irthday dear Sta-a-a-a-acy, happy birthday to you!'

Then they all applauded and someone put the music on and James asked me to dance with him.

So we danced to a couple of songs. Then Amanda danced with me. And then Cheryl danced with me. The room was totally packed and everyone seemed to be having a really great time. I didn't know very many of them, but everyone seemed to be enjoying themselves.

Maybe having Amanda arrange everything hadn't been such a bad idea after all.

And then something struck me.

I edged my way over to where Amanda was dancing with James. I tugged on her sleeve.

'Where are Pippa and Fern?' I yelled above the noise of the music.

Amanda grabbed my hands and spun me around. 'Are you having a good time?' she shouted with a huge smile. 'Can I arrange a great party or what?'

'Pippa!' I hollered. 'Fern! Where?'

'Don't worry about them,' Amanda shouted. 'Enjoy yourself!'

I danced for a while longer, then I squirmed my way over to the doorway and popped out of the living room like a cork out of a bottle. Phew! It was hot in there. A few people were hanging out in the hall, talking and eating.

I went into the kitchen. The table was covered in party snacks and little pizzas and dips and heaps of other stuff. Mom was sitting in a corner, nibbling a stick of celery and talking to one of the boys that I didn't know.

At that distance from the stereo, a person could speak without having to yell at the top of their voice.

The Unknown Party-Guest wandered off and Mom put her arm around my waist.

'Are you having a good time?' she asked.

I nodded. I was still a little breathless from all the dancing I'd been doing.

'I haven't noticed many of your friends here,' Mom said. 'Are they coming later?'

'Pippa and Fern should be here,' I said.

'Uh-huh? And what about your other school friends?'

'Uh, Amanda didn't invite them,' I said.

Mom frowned. 'Run that past me again?'

I explained why none of my classmates had been invited.

Mom looked kind of annoyed.

'This is *your* party, Stacy,' Mom said.

'Amanda should have let you invite the people you wanted to be with. I'm going to have a word with that girl.'

'Don't, Mom,' I said. 'I'm enjoying myself, honest. And Pippa and Fern will be here soon.'

I picked up a paper plate of food and went back into the living room. The dancing was getting even wilder, and I had to keep to the walls or I'd have been flattened into the carpet.

'Come on,' Rachel yelled, grabbing my arm and hauling me into the middle of the room.

It wasn't easy trying to keep track of my plate while everyone was going up and down around me like a warehouse full of exploding jack-in-the-boxes. When really popular songs played everyone would sing along at the top of their voices. I joined in, too, even though I wouldn't have minded the music being a little quieter. I mean, dancing is OK for a while, but I kind of like to talk to people, too. And talking was one thing you *couldn't* do in there.

I fought my way out into the hall. A whole hour had gone by and Pippa and Fern still hadn't shown up. I felt really upset about that. I'd hoped the three of us could make friends again today.

I sat on the stairs for a breather. There were a couple of boys I didn't know, standing talking at the side of the stairs with their backs to me.

They were talking about boring stuff mostly, but my ears pricked up when I heard one of them say, 'What's the name of Amanda's little sister? The kid whose party this is supposed to be?'

'Beats me,' said the other one. 'Tracy, I think. Or Susie.' And he laughed. 'Who cares?'

I stood up and leaned over the banister rail. 'Excuse me,' I said, 'but I think my mom and dad care. If they'd wanted me to be called *Susie* or *Tracy*, then they wouldn't have named me *Stacy*!'

They looked at me kind of sheepishly.

'And I'm not a kid,' I finished up. 'I'm eleven on Monday.'

I marched upstairs before they had the chance to say anything back. Judging from the embarrassed look on their faces, it was going to take them some time to come up with anything *to* say.

This party full of people I hardly knew was getting me down. And those two boys had really annoyed me. I wanted to know what had happened to Pippa and Fern. I needed some *friends*.

I went into Mom and Dad's bedroom and

picked up the phone. I pressed out Pippa's number.

'Hello?' It was Mrs Kane's voice.

'Hi, Mrs Kane. It's Stacy,' I said. 'Is Pippa there, please?'

'Stacy?' Mrs Kane sounded really surprised. 'Where are you?'

'At home,' I said.

'You shouldn't be at home!' Mrs Kane said. 'You should be at Fern's house!'

'I should?' I said. 'Why?'

'Didn't your sister give you Pippa's message?' Mrs Kane asked. 'I know for sure Pippa called your house this morning. She spoke to Amanda.'

DING! I suddenly remembered! The call Mom had mentioned. The one Amanda had answered. I'd totally forgotten to ask her about it. And she'd totally forgotten to tell me about it.

It had been from Pippa.

'I didn't get any message,' I said.

'Oh, heavens!' Mrs Kane said. 'Look, Stacy, Pippa and Fern are expecting you over at Fern's house. In fact, they were expecting you over an hour ago!'

'But, I'm – '

'Look, Stacy,' Mrs Kane interrupted, 'I really think you should get over to Fern's house as quick as you can! Oh, and happy birthday!'

The phone went dead.

I sat on my parents' bed with my brain doing cartwheels. The floor under my feet was vibrating from the party music and I could hear people laughing and shouting. And over at Fern's house Pippa and Fern were expecting me.

The big question was: If Amanda had invited them to my party, why were they expecting me somewhere *else*?

Yeah, if Amanda *had* invited them.

Chapter Thirteen

I met James on the stairs.

'What's wrong, Stacy?' he asked. 'You look really mad.'

'You bet I am,' I growled. 'I'm going to beat Amanda to a pulp! I've found out what she did!'

James looked at me. 'You found out?' he said.

'Darned right, I did!' I said.

'I told Amanda you'd figure it out in the end,' James said. 'But she was only trying to cheer you up, Stacy. She wouldn't have done it if she didn't really care about you.'

I stared at him. 'What are you talking about?'

He gave me an anxious kind of look. 'Uh, what are *you* talking about, Stacy?'

'I'm talking about Amanda not inviting Pippa and Fern,' I said. 'Even though I told her over and over again that I wanted them to come.'

'Oh!'

'So,' I said, suspiciously, 'what were *you* talking about?'

'Oh, nothing,' James said. 'I really need to go to the bathroom, Stacy. I'll catch you later.'

Now, that was what I'd call a weird conversation. What was it that James had thought I'd figured out? And how did Amanda *caring* about me come into it?

Well, there was only one way to find out. And that was to ask Amanda.

I went down the stairs. A song called 'Interstellar Fella' was blasting out. Everyone was singing along and jumping around in there like fish in a net. I could just about see the top of Amanda's head, way over on the other side of the room. I'd need a bulldozer to get through to her. And even if I did she wouldn't be able to hear a word I was saying.

I decided Amanda could wait. I tore a sheet of paper out of the telephone notepad.

Mom, I wrote, *I've gone to Fern's house. Back soon. Love, Stacy xx*

I tacked the note on to the bottom rail of the banister. That would stop Mom from worrying if she noticed I was missing. I was pretty sure that no one *else* in the house would miss me.

I slipped out through the front door and

went around to the side of the house to pick up my bike.

It was only a ten-minute ride to Fern's house.

I tried to work out what I'd say when I got there.

'Hey, can we forget about all the stupid stuff that's been going on recently? I just want us to be friends again.'

That was what I *really* wanted to say. And I kind of hoped that Pippa and Fern felt the same.

Of course they do, I thought to myself as I turned the corner and cycled into Fern's street. *Why else would they have called to ask me to come around here, if not to make friends again?*

I parked my bike and rang the front doorbell.

Mrs Kipsak opened the door.

'Hi,' I said. 'Is Fern home?'

'Stacy, for heaven's sake,' Mrs Kipsak said, almost dragging me into the house. 'Where on earth have you been?'

'I only just found out that Pippa called,' I explained. 'What happened was – '

'Never mind,' Mrs Kipsak said. 'You're here now. Better late than never. You'd better go right on in. They've started without you, I'm afraid.'

'Started what?' I asked, as Mrs Kipsak pushed me along the hall towards the big spare room at the back of their house.

'They're all in there,' Mrs Kipsak said.

Mrs Kipsak went into another room. *All?* What did she mean by '*all*'?

And then I heard it. Music and laughter and yells and shrieks, all coming from the back room. It sounded like there was a regular riot going on in there. I mean, I know Fern can be loud, but that was ridiculous.

There was something on the door. Some ripped edges of taped-up paper where something had been torn down. And the *something* was lying on the floor. Three sheets of paper, joined together so that they made a banner.

I bent down and turned the taped-together pieces of paper over so I could read what was written on the other side.

HAPPY BIRTHDAY, STACY! PARTY TIME! SURPRISE!!!

My stomach crashed down into the soles of my shoes.

That explained the noise in there! Fern and Pippa had organized a surprise party for me.

I stood up and opened the door.

All my friends from school were there. They were playing a really crazy game of Twister. The room was decorated with streamers and balloons. The table was covered with food and drinks. Everyone was laughing and shouting.

All these people had come to a surprise birthday party for me. All these people that I was too grown-up and sophisticated to invite to my own party. All my *friends*.

I felt awful! I felt so awful that I just wanted to crawl away into a corner and hide.

It was Denise di Novi who saw me first.

'Stacy!' she yelled.

Everything stopped. It was kind of like one of those cowboy movies where a guy walks into a saloon and everyone just stares at him in total silence.

I couldn't think of a single thing to say.

Fern hauled herself out from the tangle of arms and legs on the Twister sheet and glared at me.

'Well,' she said in a really icy voice, 'look what the cat finally dragged in!'

Chapter Fourteen

'Happy birthday for Monday, Stacy,' said a small, squashed voice in the total silence that followed what Fern had said to me.

I looked around to see where the voice had come from. It had come from little Larry Franco, from right at the bottom of the heap of Twister players.

'Thanks,' I gulped. 'I'm . . . I . . .' I looked helplessly around the room at all those faces staring at me. 'I didn't *know*,' I said. 'I only just . . . my sister . . . it wasn't . . . I never . . .'

'What do *you* want?' Fern asked.

I had felt awful before, but now I felt so bad it just wasn't true. I'd never heard Fern sound so spiteful.

'Oh, Stacy!' Pippa said. 'How *could* you?'

'Amanda didn't *tell* me,' I said in desperation. 'Honest! I came over as soon as I found out.' I could feel tears prickling in my eyes like needles.

'Just go away, Stacy!' Fern said.

I swallowed hard.

'It's not my fault!' I choked.

'Oh, right!' Fern snapped. 'And I guess it's not your fault that none of us were invited to the party at your house.'

They knew about the other party! *How* did they know?

Fern stepped forwards and gave me a push. 'Get lost. Stacy. Go back to your new friends.'

That did it. If I'd stayed there another *second* I'd have burst out crying right there in front of them all.

I ran out. Tears were pouring down my face as I stumbled along the hall and yanked the front door open. I was horribly hot all over and I could feel my cheeks burning as I ran out and grabbed my bike.

I don't know exactly what happened. Maybe it was because I was in such a rush to get out of there, or maybe it was because that darned bike was too *small* for me, but somehow my legs got all tangled up in the frame and the next thing I knew I was sitting in the Kipsaks' drive with my bike wrapped around me and my knee bleeding from a really painful scrape.

'Stacy? Are you OK?' I looked blearily up. It was Pippa.

'No!' I said. 'No, I'm not!'

'Your knee is bleeding.'

'I don't care. It can bleed all it likes. I don't *care*!'

'It'll be full of germs, Stacy,' Pippa said. 'If you don't wash it properly it'll get infected.'

'So what?'

'The infection will get worse,' Pippa said. 'And then you'll get blood poisoning and they'll have to amputate your leg.' I rubbed my hands over my eyes and stared up at her. She gave me an encouraging smile.

'And if they don't amputate in time,' she went on, 'then the blood poisoning will spread all over and you'll have to have your whole body amputated. You'll just be a *head*, Stacy. And Fern or me or someone will have to carry your head around from class to class in school and sit it on the desk facing front.' She shook her head. 'And you wouldn't want *that*.'

I couldn't help letting out a splutter of laughter through my tears.

'You're totally crazy!' I said.

'Come on inside and I'll help you clean it up,' Pippa said. She helped me to my feet. 'But keep *quiet*,' she said. 'We don't want to let Fern's mom know what happened.'

I limped back into the house and we made our way as quietly as possible to the bathroom.

'Why did you come after me?' I asked, as Pippa searched through the bathroom cabinet for some cotton wool. 'I thought you'd hate me the same as Fern does.'

'I guess I might,' Pippa said. 'But my mom always said that a person should hear both sides of the story before they make their mind up. Aha!' She took out a pack of cotton balls. 'And I guess I wanted to hear your side of the story before I decided whether to hate you or not.'

'How did you find out about the party at my house?' I asked.

'When you didn't turn up here, Fern cycled over there,' Pippa said. 'She saw the party going on through the window.' Pippa shook her head. 'If you thought she was mad just a minute ago, you should have heard her when she got back!' Pippa did a pretty good imitation of a livid Fern. ' "That rat-toad-skunk-creep-freak-monster-worm-bug-snake Stacy is having her own party over at her house! There are about a hundred people there! I hate her! I hate her for ever!" '

Pippa took a bottle of disinfectant out of the cabinet.

'You can't use that on me,' I said. 'That stuff is for putting down toilets.'

'Don't be such a wimp,' Pippa said, pouring a little of the disinfectant on to a cotton ball.

She knelt and peered in an expert kind of way at my grazed knee.

'So?' she said. 'Do you want to tell me your side of the story?' She dabbed at my knee.

'*Yeeeeeyowwww!*' I shrieked. It felt like someone had whacked my knee with a red-hot poker. 'Pippa!'

'Quit yelling,' Nurse Pippa said. 'If it's hurting it proves it's doing you good.'

'What are you *talking* about! It's killing me!'

'That's the good germs fighting the bad germs,' Doctor Pippa said calmly. 'The good germs are giving those bad germs a real hard time. That's how these things work.'

'Says who?'

'Says *me*,' Surgeon General Pippa Kane said cheerfully. She stood up. 'Now I need to find some kind of big bandage or something.'

'Maybe we ought to let Mrs Kipsak take a look at it,' I said, I still wriggling and squirming from the pain.

'I know what I'm doing,' Pippa said. (Pippa *always* says that. And you can count the number of times she really *does* know what she's doing on the fingers of one *ear*! I mean, like, *never*!)

Pippa found a bandage and started wrapping it around my knee. 'Well?' she said. 'Why weren't we invited to your party?'

I looked down at her and I felt like crying all over again.

'I don't *know* why,' I said miserably. 'I really don't. Things just kind of got out of control. Cindy went away, and you were spending all your time with Andy, and Fern was only interested in talking about her job. And I *know* I was always moaning about Cindy not being around any more, and I guess it must have gotten really boring to listen to.'

'It was worse than boring,' Pippa said. 'You made it sound like now Cindy was gone you didn't have a friend in the *world*. Like Fern and me didn't *count*.'

'Oh!' I was really shocked. 'No! That's not true. That's not how I meant it at all.'

'That's how it sounded, Stacy,' Pippa said. 'And then you didn't want to do that project with us. And then you started hanging around with your sister and her Bimbo friends.' She looked up at me. 'We were really hurt by that.'

'Ouch!'

'Sorry. I've got to tie it tight or it'll slip down.' Pippa reeled off some gauze and started wrapping it around and around my knee.

'I never meant to upset you,' I said. I tried to explain to Pippa how I'd wanted to try and get back to being really close friends with Amanda. And how it had all gone kind of wrong when Amanda had insisted on organizing my party.

'I should have *made* her invite all of my friends,' I said. 'I told her to invite you and Fern.'

'That's the first I've heard of it,' said a voice from the bathroom door. The door opened and Fern walked in. She didn't look quite so angry any more.

'Yeah,' I said, 'I found out she didn't invite you when I phoned Pippa's house and Pippa's mom said you were expecting me *here*.'

'There,' Pippa said from her crouch on the floor. 'All done! Good as new, as my mom would say.' She patted my bandaged and heavily taped-up knee. It hurt!

'Ow!'

'Oops! Sorry,' Pippa said.

I looked up at Fern. 'I've been really stupid,' I said.

'You can say that again,' Fern said.

'I've been really stupid,' I said with a hopeful grin.

'You can say that again.' Fern grinned back at me.

'I've been really – '

'Guys!' Pippa interrupted. 'Can we quit the dumb jokes?'

I stood up. My knee felt like it was trapped in a vice. Pippa sure had made sure it wouldn't slip. There was so much bandage and tape around my knee that it looked like I was wearing a football knee-pad.

'I'm really sorry,' I said to both of them. 'I've been stupid and thoughtless and totally selfish and pig-headed and dumb and . . .'

'Idiotic?' Pippa suggested.

'Bimbo-ish?' Fern added.

'Yeah,' I said. 'All of them. I just got kind of carried away with the idea that I needed to *change* myself. It was all that dumb Charles Darwin's fault! If I hadn't read all that stuff about adapting and surviving then I wouldn't have had to put up with Amanda's airheaded Bimbo friends for all that time.'

'How do you work that out?' Pippa said.

'I thought you two were changing,' I explained. 'And I thought I needed to change, too. And Amanda said that being eleven meant I had to start acting like a grown-up.'

Fern laughed. 'Oh, sure!' she said. 'Just like she does!'

'We thought you were turning into a Bimbo,' Pippa said. 'We really did!'

'I wasn't,' I insisted. 'You can't believe how

boring they are! I was going out of my mind listening to all the junk they blab about. And if I ever tried to talk about anything interesting, they'd just ignore me.'

'So you didn't like being with them?' Pippa asked.

'You've got to be kidding!' I said. 'I want to be with *you* again. I want things to be just the way they always were.' I looked anxiously at them. 'I want us to be *friends*.'

'I don't know,' Fern said. She looked at Pippa. 'I mean, do we really want to hang around with a yucky eleven-year-old?'

'I won't be a yucky eleven-year-old,' I promised. 'I'll be just the same as I always was!'

Fern laughed. 'You mean a yucky *ten*-year-old?'

'I promise to try to be less yucky in future,' I said. 'Is it a deal?'

'Do you promise you won't talk about Cindy going to California as if it was the end of the *world* any more?' Pippa asked.

'Yes. I promise.'

'And do you promise to make fun of the Bimbos like in the old days?' Fern asked.

'You bet!'

'In that case, I guess we can put up with you for a while longer,' Pippa said. 'I just hope you haven't caught any nasty Bimbo diseases. Like, loss of *brain*.'

'My brain's just fine,' I said. 'Can we forget the last few days? Can we be friends again?'

Pippa and Fern and I all hugged one another. You wouldn't believe how relieved I felt! The three of us were friends again! That was all that mattered.

'Your surprise birthday party is waiting for you,' Fern said, opening the bathroom door for me and bowing.

'And the first thing you're going to have to do,' Pippa said, 'is explain all that stuff about the other party to everyone.'

'Yeah,' Fern said. 'And you'd better hope they're as understanding about it as *we* were.'

'They will be,' Pippa said. 'Once Stacy tells them it was all Amanda's idea.'

They led me along the hall. Everyone was sitting around in the back room as if they were in a doctor's waiting room.

'Hi, again, guys,' I said. They all looked at me. 'I just want to start by saying I'm really, really glad you're all my friends.'

'Does this mean the party can start up again?' Andy Melniker asked. 'Is everything OK now?'

'It sure is!' Fern said. 'Everything is just fine!'

Chapter Fifteen

You know, sometimes it takes a big thing like the bust-up I'd had with Fern and Pippa for a person to realize who their real friends are.

Everyone at Fern's surprise party had bought me a present for my birthday. Even Larry, who hardly ever says a word to anyone, bought me a pen that wrote in four different colours when you pressed different levers.

Typical Fern wrapped my present in about fifteen sheets of paper and taped it up so I took ten minutes to get into it. It was a pair of carved stone mice, sitting up and reading books.

'They're beautiful,' I said, holding them up in my hand so everyone could see them.

'I know you usually collect pigs and frogs,' Fern said, 'but I thought your collection needed to expand.'

'So did I,' Pippa said, handing me her present. It was tube-shaped and quite heavy. I carefully peeled the wrapping off. It was a penguin! A wooden penguin with a white bib like a waiter in an expensive restaurant. It even had its beak in the air in a really snooty way.

'Snodgrass!' I said.

'Huh?'

'He's called Snodgrass,' I explained. 'You can tell right away by the expression on his face.'

'Sure thing, Stacy,' Fern said.

Then I opened all my other presents. There was a music tape from Denise, and some writing paper and envelopes from Andy and lots of really nice things from the others. I felt kind of overwhelmed by it all. (Now, I hope I'm not a greedy person, but I had noticed that not *one* of the people at my *official* birthday party had brought me even a stick of gum!)

'And now,' Fern announced, jumping on to her bed and bouncing up and down with her arms waving in the air, 'it's *party* time!'

* * *

I had such a good time. We played the kind of silly-but-fun games that Amanda and her gang would have turned their noses up at. And then Fern put on a tape of old music that had belonged to her grandma, and tried to show

132

us how to do square-dancing. She stood on the table and yelled instructions.

'Take your partner by the hand,' she hollered above the music. 'Swing her round and dance to the left! Do-si-do and away you go! No, wait! Swing her to the right. Uh, promenade, guys. No, wait a minute! That's not right!'

Well, either Fern was the worst square-dance caller in the business, or we were the worst square-dancers, because we always seemed to end up in one big heap in the middle of the floor.

In the end Fern just started making stuff up.

'Take your partner by the toe! Swing her round and let her go! Out through the window, do-si-do!'

The party started to break up after that. It was still light outside so most people made their own way home. But Mrs Kipsak gave Pippa and me a lift in the car.

'Thanks, guys,' I said as the car came to a halt outside my house. 'That was the best party *ever.*'

Mrs Kipsak helped me haul my bike out of the trunk. I waved until they had driven out of sight, then I wheeled my bike up to the side of the house. I had all my presents in a bag.

I went in through the back door. There were a few people standing around talking in the kitchen. The table looked like a plague of locusts had been across it.

The music was a lot quieter than when I had left. A few people were still dancing, but most of them were sitting around. Natalie was sitting on the stairs, talking on the phone.

'Have you seen my mom?' I asked her.

She shrugged.

Did you notice I've been missing for the past three hours? I thought. *No, you didn't!*

Amanda came running down the stairs.

'Hi, Stacy!' she said. 'Where have you been?'

Wow! *She'd* noticed I hadn't been there all afternoon. Put out the flags!

'Well, actually,' I said, 'I've been at a totally brilliant party.'

'Great,' Amanda said. 'I'm glad you've enjoyed yourself.' She stepped over Natalie and ran into the living room. 'Come on, you guys!' she shouted. 'Let's do some more dancing!'

I went in search of my mom. She wasn't upstairs. So, she had to be down in the basement. I found her stretched out in her chair. She had her eyes closed and she was wearing headphones.

I shook her.

'No, Amanda,' she said without opening her eyes. 'I am not driving down to the store for more food!'

'It's me,' I said.

She sat up and took her headphones off.

'Well,' she said with a big smile, 'I wonder how many girls get two birthday parties thrown for them on the same day?' She laughed. 'I got your note, honey,' she explained. 'I called Fern's house and Fern's mom told me all about the surprise party. Did you have a good time?'

'I had a totally brilliant time,' I said. 'And I got loads of presents.'

Mom smiled. 'Tell me all about it,' she said. 'And you can explain why you've got that huge bandage on your knee at the same time!'

She cleared a space on her desk and I sat up there and told her all about the party. I also told her about the strange couple of weeks I'd had. The weeks when I thought I needed to grow up.

'So you've made friends with Pippa and Fern again?' Mom asked.

'Yeah,' I said. 'Better than ever. I don't think I'm going to bother trying to be more grown-up any more. It doesn't seem to *work* too well.'

'Didn't I tell you not to try too hard?' Mom said.

'I guess,' I said.

'Anyway, I'm partly to blame for all this,' Mom said. 'I told Amanda to be extra-nice to you because you were so down about Cindy. And it was my idea for her to organize the party for you. Not that I expected it to end up like *this*!'

I laughed. 'I guess she *meant* well,' I said.

'Hmmm!' Mom said. 'Maybe.'

'I don't think anyone even noticed I'd gone,' I said.

Mom looked closely at me. 'Do you mind about that?' she asked.

'No,' I said with a laugh. 'I didn't even *know* half of them. And the ones I *do* know aren't my idea of a good time. I mean, I love Amanda, and all that, but she's real hard work to be friends with. And her friends are even *worse*.' I looked anxiously at my mom. 'Does that sound terrible?'

'Not at all,' Mom said. 'I bet she feels just the same about you. Just because you're sisters, it doesn't mean you have to be like two peas in a pod.' Mom stood up. 'Anyway,' she said, 'I guess it's about time we started bringing this birthday party of yours to a finish. Your dad will be home in half an hour with

Sam, and I'd kind of like the place to look a little less wrecked by then.'

'I'll help clean up,' I said.

'Oh, no, you won't!' Mom said. 'Amanda and her pals can do all the cleaning up. That'll be her punishment for using your birthday as an excuse for throwing her *own* party!'

★ ★ ★

By the time Dad and Sam got home, everyone except for Amanda, Cheryl, Natalie and Rachel had gone home. The four of them were rushing around like hyperactive hornets, clearing up under Mom's supervision.

But the best part of it all was that I was lying on the living-room couch watching TV while they were working. I saw them give me sour-faced looks every now and then, but none of them said anything. I didn't actually *hear* what was said, but I knew Mom had given them a good talking-to in the kitchen.

When everything had been tidied and cleaned and washed up and put away, the three Bimbos went home. (Hey! I can call them Bimbos again now that I don't have to pretend I like them!)

Dad was upstairs putting Sam to bed and Mom was doing something in the kitchen.

Amanda came and flopped down next to me on the couch.

'Mom says I'm supposed to apologize to you about not inviting Pippa and Fern like I promised I would,' she said.

'Amanda,' I asked, 'how come you *never* apologize for anything unless Mom tells you to?'

'I was going to apologize *anyway*,' Amanda said. 'It's just that Mom mentioned it before I got the chance.'

'So whose apology is this?' I asked.

'Mine!' Amanda said.

'Sure?'

'Yes, I'm sure.'

'In that case,' I said, 'apology accepted.'

'But, the thing is,' Amanda continued, 'you can see why I *didn't* invite them, can't you? I mean, they wouldn't have fitted in with all the other people at all. They wouldn't have had a good time.'

'It's OK,' I said. 'Forget about it. You don't have to explain.'

Amanda looked at me, her forehead wrinkled. 'You *did* enjoy yourself, didn't you? I know I kind of lost track of you during the afternoon. And I know it ended up looking like it was a party for *my* friends, but it wasn't *meant* to be like that.' She nudged me. 'Did you have a good time at all? Huh? Stacy? Did you?'

'Chill out, Amanda,' I said. 'I can honestly say that I spent this afternoon at the best party I've *ever* been to.'

'Really?' Amanda looked relieved. 'Honestly?'

'Cross my heart and hope to get stuck overnight in an elevator with Rachel Goldstein,' I said solemnly.

'Huh?'

I grinned. 'I was trying to think of the absolute *worst* thing in the world,' I explained. 'Maybe I should have said, "stuck in an elevator with Natalie Smith and having to listen to her talking about herself" – which is all she ever *does* talk about!'

'Stacy!'

'Or stuck in an elevator with Cheryl,' I said thoughtfully. 'Now *that* would be a total nightmare! Oh, I don't know, though. It'd give me plenty of time to tell her what a total *dork* she is!'

Amanda looked shocked. 'I thought you *liked* my friends now.'

'Tell me one thing, Amanda,' I said. 'Why did they start being nice to me all of a sudden? I mean, it was kind of creepy. Especially Cheryl. I know Cheryl doesn't like me at all, but she was trying really hard to make like she did. So, what was the deal?'

Amanda shrugged. 'OK,' she said. 'Put the handcuffs on me! I was trying to help, OK? Mom told me to be nice to you because you were missing Cindy. She said being nice to you would show how emotionally mature I'd become, whatever *that* means.' She shrugged. 'I told the guys to be nice to you, too.'

Got it! *That* was what James had been talking about earlier when he'd said Amanda had only done *it* because she cared about me! She'd actually managed to talk the Bimbos into being nice to me. Wow! Now that's what I call an achievement!

No wonder Cheryl had to be kicked under the table every now and then. And no wonder Rachel seemed to be giggling about *nothing* all the time.

I flung my arms around Amanda's neck.

'Amanda!' I said. 'You're the greatest sister in the world!'

'I am?' she gasped.

'You bet!'

'Stacy, you're strangling me.'

'Sorry.' I let go of her. 'I just want you to know I really appreciate it,' I said. 'But, well, could you tell them not to bother any more? I think I prefer it when we don't get along.'

'I see,' Amanda said. 'So you don't want to grow up after all, huh?'

'Oh, I'm going to grow up, OK,' I said. 'I just don't want to grow up like your Bimbo friends.'

'Well, of all the – '

'Face it, Amanda,' I said. 'You're a really great sister sometimes, but the things you and your friends talk about are totally and utterly boring!'

'Are you two bickering?' Mom asked as she walked in.

'Stacy just called my friends boring,' Amanda said. 'She's got to be kidding! If we're going to start a big-league *boring* contest, I think the names *Fern* and *Pippa* should be at the top of the list!'

'Get out of here!' I said. 'Cheryl and Natalie could win medals in the Boring Olympics!'

'Hold it right there!' Mom said. 'When will you two get it into your heads that just because people don't interest *you* it doesn't mean they're boring?'

'But – ' we both said.

'But nothing!' Mom said. 'I don't want to hear another word about it! Amanda has her friends, and you, Stacy, have yours. No one is asking you all to hug and kiss one another every time you meet, but you've got to learn to be more tolerant!'

I didn't say another word.

But that didn't mean Cheryl and Natalie and Rachel *weren't* boring. It just meant I was too polite to mention it!

★ ★ ★

'Why do you have a bandage on your knee?' Amanda asked me a little while later.

'Because I hurt it,' I said. 'I fell off my bike.'

'I don't remember seeing it when you were getting ready for the party.'

'I didn't have it then.'

Amanda gave me a strange look.

'So, you did it *afterwards*? Between getting ready for the party and now?'

'That's right.'

'But you've been at the party all afternoon,' Amanda said. 'How could you have fallen off your bike?'

'Amanda,' I said with a grin. 'I'm afraid that's just going to be one of life's big mysteries for you.'

Amanda never found out what had happened. And I never told her about the surprise party I'd been to at Fern's house, either!

Chapter Sixteen

I had a long talk on the phone with Cindy the next morning. I told her everything that had happened recently. And I mean *everything*. That was the great thing with Cindy and me: we always told each other all those little secrets that we didn't tell anyone else.

Like those times when you know you've behaved badly and feel really ashamed of yourself. Or times when you do things that are so *dumb* that you feel like crawling under a rock and never showing your face again.

And I sure had been dumb over the last couple of weeks.

I even told Cindy about how jealous I was of her new friend Shannon.

'That is so silly,' Cindy said. 'Shannon is just a *friend*. *You're* still my best ever friend. Don't you remember what you wrote on my going away card? "Friendship doesn't count the miles." It's true! You're always going to be the best friend I'll ever have.'

'And you're always going to be my best friend ever!' I said.

'That's right!'

I felt a whole lot better after the call to Cindy. It was great to know we could still talk to each other like that, even if it was only once a week.

After lunch, I was sitting in the kitchen writing out a list of all the birthday presents I'd gotten so far, with my new four-coloured pen from Larry. Mom was upstairs giving Sam a bath and Dad was watching motor-racing on TV in the living room.

The front-door bell rang. It was Cheryl.

'Hi, Stacy,' Cheryl said with a big beaming smile.

'Amanda's upstairs,' I said.

'Did you have a good time yesterday?' she asked. 'I thought it was a really neat party! Hey, a bunch of us are going over to the Happy Donut. Do you want to come, too?'

I looked at her. 'Cheryl,' I said, 'you don't have to keep it up any more. Amanda told me all about it. I really appreciate the effort, but you can quit it now.'

Cheryl gave me a puzzled smile.

'I know Amanda told you to be nice to me,' I said. 'It must have been real hard work for

144

you, and I'm grateful, and all that. But you can *stop* now, OK?'

She stood there looking at me for a few seconds.

'Really?' she said.

'Uh-huh.' I nodded.

'*Pheee-hewww!*' She let out a long whistling breath. 'So you won't be hanging around us all the time any more?'

'Nope,' I said.

'Thank goodness for that!' Cheryl said. She put her hand on my shoulder. 'I mean, I did my best, Stacy, but, let's face it, you are one boring little kid.'

I smiled sweetly at her. 'Well, thanks, Cheryl, 'I said. 'And you are an airheaded Bimbo with all the charm of a squashed bug.'

'If I'd had to spend one more day being nice to you,' Cheryl said, 'I'd have gone out of my mind!'

'What mind?' I said. 'There's so much empty space between your ears, they could build a supermarket in there.'

Amanda hung over the banister.

'What are you guys doing?' she called down.

'Getting things back to normal!' I said.

'Yeah,' Cheryl said. 'And not a moment too soon!'

She marched upstairs and I went back into the kitchen.

Benjamin was sitting on my birthday present list, grooming himself with one leg in the air.

'Well, Benjamin,' I said with a happy sigh as I sat down, 'I'd say this has been a pretty successful weekend so far. I've had a good talk with Cindy; I've sorted things out with Fern and Pippa, and I've insulted Cheryl Ruddick.' I leaned forward and stroked his head.

'And tomorrow,' I said, 'I get all the rest of my presents!'

★ ★ ★

'Happy birthday!'

Amanda came bursting into my room with a breakfast tray in her hands.

I sat up, still only half-awake as she dumped the tray across my legs and opened the blind.

'Thanks,' I said with a big yawn. As well as breakfast, there was a pile of cards on the tray and a small package.

'Eat up quickly,' Amanda urged. 'There are more things for you downstairs.' She picked up the package and waggled it under my nose. 'It's postmarked "California",' she said.

'From Cindy!' I said. I tore the packing off. Inside was a box. And in the box, wrapped in tissue, was a little crystal statue of a leaping dolphin.

There was a card as well: *To my best friend*.

I stuffed some toast in my mouth and started opening my cards. There were nine. Including the cards I'd gotten at my surprise party, I was now up to twenty-three cards!

'Come down and open the rest,' Amanda said, almost dragging me out of bed.

Mom, Dad and Sam were waiting in the living room.

'Happy birthday!'

'Oh, wow!' I said as I saw what was waiting in there for me with a ribbon tied around the handlebars. 'Oh, wow! Wow! Wow! My *bike*!'

I had mentioned once or twice that my bike was getting a little small for me, but Mom and Dad hadn't said anything, so I'd kind of thought they hadn't been listening.

But they *had*! It was a real mountain bike with fifteen gears.

I gave Mom and Dad a big hug. 'It's even my favourite colour!' I said, as I climbed on to test it for size. It had a bright yellow frame. 'It's perfect!' I said. 'Thanks! It's just *perfect*!'

I dived into the other presents. I got a really neat saddle-bag from Aunt Susie and a safety helmet from Laine, so the bike must have been planned for ages.

And I got a huge jigsaw of two tigers in the jungle and a big book on cats with loads of pictures in it.

'Open mine!' Amanda said.

She'd bought me a boxed-set book, audio-tape and video all about Yellowstone Park.

'And this is from Grandma and Grandad Whittle,' Mom said. 'They asked me what I thought you'd like.' She smiled. 'I hope I got it right.'

It was small portable tape recorder.

'Now you can send Cindy recorded messages as well as letters,' Mom said.

'That's totally brilliant!' I said. 'This has got to be the best birthday I've ever had!'

*   *   *

When I met up with Fern and Pippa at school, it was as if we'd never been mad at each other. In fact, I got told off by Ms Fenwick for whispering to them during class. And that hadn't happened for *days*. It seemed like things were just about back to normal.

I went up to the cafeteria with Fern. We picked up our trays and walked over to our usual table. No more sitting with the Bimbos for me!

We had just sat down when Pippa and Andy

Melniker came over with their trays and sat with us.

I felt a tiny twinge of irritation that Pippa was still spending time with Andy. I guess I wanted it to just be the three of us. I didn't *mind* Andy, but I did feel like he was kind of in the way.

'Do you mind Andy sitting with us?' Pippa asked.

'It's a free country,' Fern mumbled through a mouthful of sandwich.

'I don't mind,' I said.

Pippa looked at him. 'Do you want me to tell them?'

'No,' Andy said. 'I will.'

Fern and I looked at him. Tell us what? He looked a little awkward.

'Go on,' Pippa urged him.

Andy took a deep breath. 'I guess everyone will find out sooner or later,' he said, staring down at his tray. 'My mom and dad have split up.'

'Oh, no,' I said. 'That's awful! That's so awful!'

Fern just looked at him as if she couldn't think of anything to say.

'Would you like my yoghurt?' she said. 'It's strawberry. It'll make you feel better.' She reached over and put it in front of him.

'Thanks,' he said.

'Don't mention it,' Fern said, glancing across at me as if to say, *What do we do now?*

'Andy told me about it a couple of weeks ago,' Pippa said. 'But he didn't want anyone else to know. I guess he knew I'd understand how he was feeling.' Pippa's mom and dad had got divorced a couple of years ago. I remembered how upset she'd been at the time.

'Maybe they'll get back together?' Fern said.

'I don't think so,' Andy said, fishing around in the yoghurt with his spoon. 'I think it's pretty final.'

I watched as Andy scooped a chunk of strawberry off his spoon and ate it with his fingers.

'Do you always do that?' I asked.

'Huh?' He looked at me.

'Cindy used to do that,' I said. 'She used to pick out the chunks from yoghurt exactly the same way you just did.'

'I didn't even know I was doing it,' Andy said.

'Whoo! Spooky!' Fern said. 'It must be the psychic spirit of Cindy doing weird things to Andy's mind because he's sitting in her place.'

I thought maybe we should take Andy's mind off his troubles. I took out my brand-new tape recorder.

'We can send Cindy a message from all of us!' Pippa said. 'That is such a cool present!'

I said a few words, then handed the tape recorder to Fern. She was still thinking about what to say when we were interrupted.

'Well, well,' said a screechy, sarcastic voice, 'if it isn't the Nerd Queen of Indiana and all her nerdy little nerdlings.'

'Either there's a hyena loose in the cafeteria,' I said, 'or that's got to be some kind of mega-Bimbo.' I looked around. 'Oh, I was right on *both* counts! Hi, Cheryl!'

'Gone back to your kiddie pals, huh, Stacy?' Cheryl said. 'Was life a little too exciting for you with the big girls?'

'Big girls, bean-brains,' Fern said.

'Oh, and *look*!' Cheryl said, smirking at Andy. 'A brand-new nerdling to make up for the nerdling that got lost. Isn't that *sweet*!'

'Cindy didn't get lost,' I said. 'She went to California to get away from *you*! Why don't you go and live in China?'

'Pass me the tape recorder,' Andy said to Fern. She handed it to him. He pressed *Record*.

'Hi, Cindy,' he said into the microphone. 'This is Andy Melniker speaking to you from deep in the African jungle. I'm out here on safari, and I've just discovered a rare spiky-haired orang-utan.' He held the recorder up to Cheryl. 'Would you like to say something for the folks back home?' he asked her.

'Get that thing out of my face!' Cheryl snapped.

'Did you hear that, Cindy?' Andy said into the microphone. 'It *spoke*! It must be the missing link between apes and human beings.'

Cheryl turned and marched off.

We all laughed.

'That was great, Andy,' I said. 'You can sit at our table all you like!'

A big grin spread across Andy's face.

'I might just take you up on that,' he said.

And he did. The four of us sat together at our special table every lunchtime from then on. I'm not saying that Andy was any kind of substitute for Cindy. Cindy will *always* be my best friend. But there was something really nice about there being four of us in the gang again.

And like Fern said, 'If Andy can come up with great anti-Bimbo cracks like the spiky-haired orang-utan gag he got Cheryl with, then he's welcome at *my* house any time!'

And Pippa and I felt exactly the same.

Stacy and Amanda are back in LITTLE
SISTER 10: SUMMER CAMP

The girls are off to camp for the summer and
the best thing about it is they're going to different ones! They just can't wait to see the back
of each other – a whole summer with no Nerd
vs Bimbo battles. But disaster strikes and
Stacy's packed off to airhead heaven – Amanda's camp! Things go from bad to worse as
Stacy discovers that Amanda's lost the plot
completely and is telling anyone who'll listen
that Stacy's not Stacy and her whole family is
famous! Confused? Stacy certainly is and her
next big dilemma is what to do about it.
Should she help Amanda, or leave her to face
the consequences on her own . . .?

To find out, check out a copy of SUMMER
CAMP, only in Red Fox.

ISBN: 0 09 968871 9 £2.99

Other great reads from **Red Fox**

Further Red Fox titles that you might enjoy reading are listed on the following pages. They are available in bookshops or they can be ordered directly from us.

If you would like to order books, please send this form and the money due to:

ARROW BOOKS, BOOKSERVICE BY POST, PO BOX 29, DOUGLAS, ISLE OF MAN, BRITISH ISLES. Please enclose a cheque or postal order made out to Arrow Books Ltd for the amount due, plus 75p per book for postage and packing to a maximum of £7.50, both for orders within the UK. For customers outside the UK, please allow £1.00 per book.

NAME_____

ADDRESS_____

_____

Please print clearly.

Whilst every effort is made to keep prices low, it is sometimes necessary to increase cover prices at short notice. If you are ordering books by post, to save delay it is advisable to phone to confirm the correct price. The number to ring is THE SALES DEPARTMENT 0171 (if outside London) 973 9000.

Other great reads from **Red Fox**

Little Sister Series by Allan Frewin Jones

LITTLE SISTER 1 – THE GREAT SISTER WAR

Meet Stacy Allen, a ten year old tomboy and a bit of a bookworm. Now meet her blue-eyed blonde sister, Amanda, just turned 13 and a fully-fledged teenager. Stacy thinks Amanda's a total airhead and Amanda calls Stacy and her gang the nerds; they have the biggest love-hate relationship of the century and that can only mean one thing – war.
ISBN 0 09 938381 0   £2.99

LITTLE SISTER 2 – MY SISTER, MY SLAVE

When Amanda starts to become a school slacker, Mom is ready to take drastic action – pull Amanda out of the cheerleading squad! So the sisters make a deal; Stacy will help Amanda with her school work in return for two whole days of slavery. But Amanda doesn't realize that when her little sister's boss, two days means 48 *whole* hours of chores – snea-kee!
ISBN 0 09 938391 8   £2.99

LITTLE SISTER 3 – STACY THE MATCHMAKER

Amanda is mad that the school Barbie doll, Judy McWilliams, has got herself a boyfriend, and to make things worse it's hunky Greg Masterson, the guy Amanda has fancied for ages. Stacy feels that it's her duty as sister to fix Amanda's lovelife and decides to play cupid and do a bit of matchmaking, with disastrous results!
ISBN 0 09 938401 9   £2.99

LITTLE SISTER 4 – COPYCAT

Cousin Laine is so coo-ol! She's a glamorous 18 year old and wears gorgeous clothes, and has got a boyfriend with a car. When Stacy and Amanda's parents go away for a week leaving Laine in charge, 13 year old Amanda decides she wants to be just like her cousin and begins to copy Laine's every move . . .
ISBN 0 09 938411 6   £2.99

Other great reads from **Red Fox**

Little Sister Series by Allan Frewin Jones

LITTLE SISTER 5 – SNEAKING OUT

Pop star Eddie Eden is *the* guy every cool teenager is swooning over and Amanda has got a mega crush on him. Amanda is in love big time and when Eddie's tour dates are announced she's desperate to see her idol – but Mom and Dad don't want her out so late. So what else is there for a love-struck girl to do but sneak out?
ISBN 0 09 938421 3   £2.99

LITTLE SISTER 6 – SISTER SWITCH

Stacy's pen pal, Craig, loves her letters and all his friends are jealous when they see her photo – so he fixes a date. This is bad news for the Allen sisters. Stacy hates her mousy hair and freckles so much that she sent him a photo of pretty Amanda. But if Stacy can persuade Amanda to swop places and be *her* for one day she might be able to keep her secret identity safe . . .
ISBN 0 09 938431 0   £2.99

Other great reads from **Red Fox**

Little Sister Series by Allan Frewin Jones

LITTLE SISTER 7 – FULL HOUSE

When Aunt Susie comes to stay Stacy and Amanda are forced to – horror of horrors – *share a room*! Naturally a territorial riot breaks out. Will they be too busy arguing with each other to notice that Mom and sister Susie are indulging in a bit of sisterly fireworks of their own?
ISBN 0 09 966121 7   £2.99

LITTLE SISTER 8 – BAD BOY

No more teen crushes, Amanda is 100% certain, it's true love with a capital 'L'. *She's* crazy over a gorgeous guy and *he's* mad about his babe, Amanda. Or is he? When Stacy spots Amanda's hunk with arch enemy, Judy MacWilliams, she decides it's time to take some sisterly action to protect Amanda from a broken heart. . .
ISBN 0 09 966641 3   £2.99

LITTLE SISTER 9 – THE NEW STACY

Something weird is happening to Stacy's girlie gang. Cindy's taken off to sunny California, Pippa's hanging out with a *guy* and Fern has disappeared from the social scene – she's become a work-a-holic! Is befriending Amanda's Bimbo pals the answer? Lonely heart Stacy decides the time has come to find out!
ISBN 0 09 966651 0   £2.99

Join the RED FOX Reader's Club

The Red Fox Reader's Club is for readers of all ages. All you have to do is ask your local bookseller or librarian for a Red Fox Reader's Club card. As an official Red Fox Reader you only have to borrow or buy eight Red Fox books in order to qualify for your own Red Fox Reader's Clubpack – full of exciting surprises! If you have any difficulty obtaining a Red Fox Reader's Club card please write to: Random House Children's Books Marketing Department, 20 Vauxhall Bridge Road, London SW1V 2SA.